On the Gulf

W9-AXZ-036

Elizabeth Spencer

ON THE GULF

University Press of Mississippi

Jackson

www.upress.state.ms.us

The University Press of Mississippi is a member of
the Association of American University Presses.

Library of Congress Cataloging-in-Publication Data

Spencer, Elizabeth, 1921–
On the gulf / Elizabeth Spencer. — 1st paperback ed.
p. cm. — (Banner books.)
ISBN 978-1-61703-684-2 (pbk. : alk. paper) —
ISBN 978-1-61703-685-9 (ebook) 1. Women—Fiction.
2. Gulf Coast (U.S.)—Fiction. I. Title.
PS3537.P4454A6 2013
813'.54—dc23   2012011629

British Library Cataloging-in-Publication Data available

TO THOMASINA
With many golden memories of that place
and the happy hours passed there.

For a beginning
let yourself be drawn like debris
to all the great bodies of water:
I will be there
asking you to help
lift up a hand of water
and reach into a time
we dream to change.

—JAMES SEAY,
from *Water Tables*

CONTENTS

INTRODUCTION
An Opening to the Sea

If I could have one part of the world back the way it used to be, I would not choose Dresden before the fire bombing, Rome before Nero, or London before the blitz. I would not resurrect Babylon, Carthage or San Francisco. Let the leaning tower lean and the hanging gardens hang. I want the Mississippi Gulf Coast back as it was before Hurricane Camille.

All through my childhood and youth, north of Jackson, up in the hills, one happy phrase comes down intact: "the coast." *They've just been to the coast ... they're going to the coast next week ... they're fishing at the coast ... they own a house at the coast ... let's go to the coast.... When? For spring holidays? next week? ... Now!*

What was magical about it? In the days I speak of, it did not have a decent beach. Strictly speaking, it was not even a sea coast. The islands that stood out in the Gulf— Horn Island, Ship Island, Cat Island and the rest—took the Gulf surf on their sandy shores: what we called "the coast" was left with a tide you could measure in inches, and a gradual silted sloping sea bottom, shallow enough to wade out in for half a mile without getting wet above the waist.

A concrete sea wall extended for miles along the beach drive, shielding the road and houses and towns it ran past from high water that storms might bring, also keeping the shore line regular. Compared to the real beaches of Southern California, or Florida, or the Caribbean islands, all this might seem not much to brag about: what was there beside the sea wall, the drive along it, the palms and old lighthouses, the spacious mansions looking out on the water, with their deep porches and outdoor stairways, their green lattice work, their moss hung oaks and sheltered gardens, the crunch of oyster shells gravelling side roads and parking lots . . . why was this so grand?

Well, it wasn't "grand," let that be admitted. Natchez was grand. New Orleans had its seductive charms securely placed in a rich Creole history. Still, nothing gave Mississippians quite the feeling of our own Gulf Coast.

We came down to it driving through plain little towns, some pretty, some not, went south of Jackson through Hattiesburg. The names come back: Mendenhall, Magee, Mount Olive, Collins, Wiggins, Perkinston. Somewhere in there was D'Lo, curiously pronounced Dee-Lo. In all of these, people of an Anglo-Saxon sameness in names and in admirable qualities, were pursuing life patterns thought out so long ago they could never be questioned since. A day or two to piece the relationships together and anyone from Carrollton or Winona or Pickens or Vaiden could pick up the same routine of life there as in the ancestral home.

But soon there was the thrilling smell of salt on the breeze increasing until suddenly there was Gulfport and straight ahead the harbor with its big ships at rest and to either side the long arms of the beach drive stretching east to Biloxi, west to Pass Christian and Bay St. Louis. There were names foreign to our ears, the mystery of these almost foreign places, easy in their openness, leaning toward the flat blue water, serene beneath the great floating clouds. That first thin breath of sea air had spread to a whole atmosphere. There was no place where it wasn't.

What to do in a car crowded with friends on holiday from school but drive straight to the water's edge and sit there breathless, not knowing which way to go first, but ready to discover.

I must have come there first with girls from around home, or friends from college in Jackson. Someone would have borrowed the family car. Occasions blur into one long sighing memory of live oaks green the year round, and the pillared white houses the trees sheltered, set along the sweep of beach drive, boxes of salt water taffy to chew on, and little screened restaurants advertising SHRIMP! ALL YOU CAN EAT FOR $1. Gumbo, too, "made fresh every day." Jax beer. Prohibition lingered for a long time inland, but the coast never paid it much attention. Names alone would tell you that they wouldn't. French and Spanish were here from the first, but Poles and Yugoslavs and Czechs had come long ago to work in the fishing industries, while the French traded and the Spanish built ships. But we wouldn't have thought of looking up their history. It was the feeling those names breathed that stirred us: Ladnier, Saucier, Legendre, Christovich, Benachi, Lameuse, Lopez, Toledano. Religion here was foreign, too: churches like Our Lady of the Gulf stood proclaiming it, with a statue of the Virgin in the wide paved entrance court, and a bare but graceful façade, facing boldly out to sea. Those who ran the restaurants, and went out in the shrimp boats, worshipped here, as did no doubt the men who waded the shallow water at night with flambeaux blazing, spears ready for flounder, and the women, too, who sat talking through the long afternoons on latticed porches. We learned that annually at Biloxi, before the shrimp boats go out to their deep sea fishing grounds, an outdoor mass is held to bless the fleet. It is a great occasion, and one of general rejoicing. These were ancient ways. Above, the white clouds mounted high, the gulls on broad white wings soared and tacked, tilting into the wind. The pelicans stroked toward land in flawless formation. Mid-afternoon in spring. Intense heat had not yet taken over, but a stillness came on, a sense of absolute suspension. The camellias were long finished, the azaleas, lingering, but past their height. Magnolia blooms starred dark green branches. Jasmine breathed in the back gardens. The moss hung breezeless. Time stood still.

We were used to staying at the Edgewater Gulf, a wonderful hotel between Gulfport and Biloxi. Its grounds were ample. I remember a cool lobby of gently turning ceiling fans, plants in white recesses, and rooms designed each with a long entrance passage facing on the sea, drawing a constant breeze through latticed doors. Parting admonitions—"Don't talk to strangers," "Be careful where you swim," "Be sure to call Sally the minute you get there"—may have sounded in our ears for a while on the way down, but vanished after Gulfport. Yet I cannot recall any serious mischief we ever got ourselves into.

Grown beyond all that and long out of school, I was to return to the coast many times over after our spring holiday frolics. A nagging sense began to persist that the coast was withholding something; I'd something yet to solve. Then I took the boat one summer and went out to Ship Island. Ship Island is the largest and best known of the coastal islands, and the only one that excursion boats go out to. It takes these little tourist ferries well over an hour to make the twelve miles or so to the island. But who is in a hurry? Someone in the pilot house will be playing an harmonica. Cold drinks and snacks are sold in the galley. The island is low and white, like a sandbar with dunes. Once ashore, the dunes seem higher: they mount up before the visitor, low hills fringed with sea oats which blow in the steady breeze. Wooden walkways climb among them. There are signs to an old fort to the west, dating from Civil War days. History will be related on the dutiful markers. An old weathered lighthouse, wooden, four-sided, gray, stands guard.

I am speaking now of 1951, the first visit I made to this spot. Like the coast itself, though, it had been mentioned so often throughout my childhood as to seem part of my own personal geography. Everyone had been to Ship Island. Picnics were talked of, summer days recalled. On that first time for me, I remember walking ahead of friends (a man I went with then, two friends of his) straight south, taking the walk through the dunes. Then, cresting, I saw it there before me, what I'd come for without knowing it: the true Gulf, no horizon to curb its expanse, spread out infinite and free, restless with tossing white caps, rushing in to foam up the beach, retreating, returning, roaring. Out there I thought, astonished, is Mexico, the Caribbean, South America. We are leaning outward to them. Everybody back there on land, all along the coast, feels this presence, whether they consciously know it or not. What was it but the distance, the leaning outward, the opening toward far-off, unlikely worlds? The beyond.

Here at the Mississippian's southernmost point of native soil, one had to recall what inland Mississippi was like, how people in its little towns (or even in larger towns like Meridian and Jackson and Columbus) related inward, to family life, kinfolks, old friendships and hatreds. How hospitably newcomers were welcomed, but how slowly accepted. Once I heard the remark: "The H-----s haven't lived here but thirty years, but look how everybody likes them!" In talk of the outside world, not much was to be accepted, nothing could be trusted to be "like us." There were Yankees "up there," we said to ourselves, looking north; the other Southern states, like neighboring counties, offered names that could be traced in and out among one's connection and might prove acceptable. There was a single Jewish family in the town where I was brought up: they had come to run the local department store, one of a chain. There was one Catholic lady, unmarried, who lived in a fine old house among some cedars. High steps went up to it from the street and a long front walk led to a white pillared porch. This lady was the object of solicitous telephone calls during the summer revival meetings that the Protestant churches took turns holding. She got some amusement from these, we had to guess; the answers she was quoted as giving sounded as if she did. "No, the Pope told me I could play bridge. I was talking to him on the phone just this morning. He said I could smoke, too, if I wanted to, and a glass of sherry wouldn't hurt anything."

In such towns people lived on stories of each other's sayings and doings, repeating and checking for the facts, speculating and measuring and fitting together the present to the past, the known to the suspected, weaving numberless patterns. It was a complex and at times beautiful society; much fine literature has been created to do it justice; but the smell of salt air did not reach it, and none can deny that it was confined and confining.

So one from those places comes to stand, in memory fixed there forever like a monument or a snapshot, on a Ship Island dune staring out to sea.

In the story of mine included here, named for the island, a young girl comes there with her summer lover, and in the sight and feel of the sea discovers her own true nature—good or bad, she finds it there, like a wonderful shell dug out of the sand. In Walker Percy's book *The Moviegoer*, we read: "You come over the hillock and your heart lifts up; your old sad music comes into the major." That's another way of saying it. But it may be that the only way of knowing it is to go there.

From the summer of 1951 to the following spring I went to live on the coast. I took a small apartment in back of a wonderful old lady's house in Pass Christian. I had begged off from teaching for a year at the University of Mississippi, and was at the coast trying to take a new start on some writing I had only vaguely in mind. How I wrote anything I don't really understand, for it was a time of many visits.

Not the least were two blessed descents of Eudora Welty from Jackson, bringing with her each time a friend she wanted me to meet. The first was Katherine Anne Porter who had given a lecture in Jackson on a series featuring Southern writers. (I had myself been asked to participate, but was unbearably shy on a platform in those days, and had declined.) Miss Porter was, as so often described, beautiful, with snow white hair. Her small figure seemed delicate without being fragile. Her features were remarkable for showing no trace of slack skin; I was reminded of the trim, spare, expressive faces that Florentine sculptors knew so well how to mold.

I had the two ladies over to my little apartment one evening. We sat and sipped drinks and talked. I will always be glad that Katherine Anne (as she insisted I call her) talked so much about herself. She felt like doing this, and she did it. Where else could I have heard her precise but soft voice say, "I would have been able to do much more, except for the many interruptions—by that I mean the time I've given to men." I think this is reasonably exact. It was honest and certainly not coy; she was anything but that. Another observation I recall: "I don't understand people who complain about art for art's sake. If we don't love her for her own sake, why else do we love her?"

She and Eudora were staying at the old Miramar Hotel, just west of Pass Christian. It was a comfortably run-down old place; I used a made-up version of it in my novel *The Salt Line*. My feeling was that people who had made a habit of coming to the coast through the years had grown used to staying there and nowhere else. I remember sitting on the floor of the large room Katherine Anne had—I think she was propped up on pillows and trying to nurse away a cold or headache—and listening to her and Eudora talk, though of what subjects I can't recall.

It was sometime after this that Elizabeth Bowen also visited Eudora. The two of them came by to see me before proceeding to New Orleans where Miss Bowen was to lecture. We planned to meet for lunch at Friendship House, a wonderfully sprawled out restaurant on the beach drive east of Gulfport, just before Biloxi. The day was mild and the broad windows looked out on the sound. And on the beach drive lined with oaks. The water lay placid and blue beyond. I remember the delightful sound of Miss Bowen's very English voice, not exactly marred by stuttering, but made a little comical when she came to speak of our wonderful b-b-buh-bourbon whisky. Or related coming into the airport of some Western city (she had been lecturing throughout the U.S.), and how she had admired those numerous neon s-s-suh-signs. I wondered at her courage to undertake lectures at all, but am told that her fine quality and her certainly imposing looks—tall, strongly built, with red hair swept back—more than made up for the flaw. I came to know that she was one of Eudora's closest friends, had invited her often for visits to Bowen's Court, the family home in County Cork, Ireland, and that they each lavished admiration on the other's work.

I also remember that the two ladies were late in appearing that day, having not started early enough from Jackson, and that I was seated in the restaurant foyer waiting for a good while when two young officers from the nearby air base came out of the bar and started to talk. Was I waiting for someone? Yes, two women friends from Jackson. Both from Mississippi? No, one was from Ireland. "Ah, a Jackson doll and an Irish babe!" When the imposing pair actually came through the door, regal in their tweeds, the air force wilted away.

During those months of sojourn on the coast, I tried every day to work, but nothing seemed to flow. I had a second novel slated to come out in the spring. Just having finished a book creates difficulties in starting another. In spare afternoons, closing up the hope of a fresh start for yet another day, I used to drive to places I loved seeing. One by one they were there for me to find and re-find, always giving off to me their air of a past which I knew had occurred, but which I had no key to opening up, could not do what a writer most enjoys, visualize with confidence what has not actually been seen.

For instance there was DeLisle, a town site inland from the beach drive, just northwest of Pass Christian. Once out of sight of water, oaks gave room to pines, the tall longleaf pines of South Mississippi, and the road, largely unpaved, was carpeted in pine needles, quietened by a mix of sand in loam. DeLisle itself was fairly populous once, and was all but entirely French, the descendants of the Acadians from Nova Scotia having settled here. French was taught in school far into this century. A plain little church, in my day, was still standing, and a few houses. The spaces where houses and stores must once have stood were peaceful savannahs, moss-hung round the edges, keeping memories not to be shared with me. A cloud of butterflies could be counted on to waft about like a length of yellow silk floating on air. A wooden bridge led over still black water, Bayou DeLisle.

A few miles beyond I would come to the really spooky place, Pine Hills, an old resort hotel, set in extensive grounds just at the head of Bay St. Louis. It was begun during a boom year, 1926, and some people around Pass Christian had told me that it never opened, thus awakening in my mind images of fabulous chateaux, villas, castles, or mansions, richly prepared for expected guests, the snow-white linens starched and spread, the place settings of china, crystal and silver all laid, the bedrooms expectant and fragrant, the staff coached, the management ready with smiles. Then—no one comes. All that is largely fantasy, of course; the hotel went down as an operating venture in the crash of 1929 and never re-opened. Until a couple of years ago, it still stood, empty and expectant.

To go there alone past the entrance gates, observe the small filling station with pumps for gas still in place, and toward the far right outbuildings of every sort standing vacant—stables? garages? servants' quarters?—the tennis courts all weedy silence, and most of all to see looming straight ahead, the massive hotel itself, windows by the hundreds with no one behind them, the curving entrance drive where no arriving guests would ever alight, no door ever swing wide to receive them—this was awesome.

It was told to me that the long room to the left of the entrance lobby had been the banquet hall. I once crept close enough to see if the tables were, as I had been told, still prepared for dinner, but I don't recall confirmation of the tale. Perhaps to anyone able actually to enter those dusky halls and cobwebbed lobbies, details would have opened out, a pen ready beside a blank registration page, a key forgotten in a cabinet for vases, one final ashtray left unemptied on a table. Who knows?

Rounding a corner of the hotel, one came suddenly into a full view of Bay St. Louis. Came only to learn that others before the hotel builders had felt the command and sweep of this site. A towering shell mound, said to be the largest on the coast, still stood for marvelling at. Even more than the hotel, it held its Indian mystery, of how it came to be put there, for what impressive purpose. At least the hotel planners had the sense to leave it alone. Perhaps they thought of it as a curiosity for the guests to look at, strolling at twilight in full evening dress before cocktails and dinner. Now both monuments—hotel and mound—stand side by side, looking out over the bay. And the bay may well be asking itself who will come next to rear a monument and pass away.

My other favorite spot to visit—far over to the east in Ocean Springs—was, in contrast, very much a going concern. The Shearwater Pottery was owned and run by the Anderson family. It wasn't all that easy to find. You had to know where to look. You reached the house from a street in Ocean Springs, having searched carefully to see a modest sign, just a little plank nailed to a tree, saying "Shearwater Pottery" and sporting the painted logo of a gull at wing. The drive to reach it wound through shaggy growth, small oaks, azaleas, Cherokee rose bushes and camellias—all looking never to have been planted or tended, part of the wild. A turn and there was the Anderson house, modest like the sign, but beautiful in its traditional Gulf Coast architecture, the gables, the slanted roof, the porch. The pottery itself was in a shed-like building. Nearby was the shop, where the various figurines designed here were displayed along with vases, jardinières, plates. The designs, taken from the natural life that lay all around, had in their movement, the humor and rhythm of their execution, a totally original quality. Since those days it has come into full light how great an artist was at work here. Locally known and protected—he evidently was the sort of eccentric people fear may come to harm—coast people during his lifetime certainly prized him. But I doubt if any friend or neighbor or visitor knew the extent, let alone the magnificence of Walter Anderson's art. He seemed, like the Lord God before him, to be creating every day, fish, fowl, plants, flowers, trees, sea and air, leaving behind him such abundance at his death that the Gulf Coast needs to find no other means to immortality.

I used to see them—him or one of his brothers, sometimes both, though which brother I never quite got straight. They were in and out of the shop, not looking so much distracted as alive to other matters than who came in to buy. Yet you could talk with them, ask questions which were cordially and briefly answered. They went about in old dungarees, canvas shoes, denim shirts, a pull-over in winter. This was right for them. I brought people there who came to visit me. Some of their figurines which I bought there—"widgets" they called them—have gone with me on many moves. A wing may break from a gull or a foot from a dancing black man, and have to be mended, but the charm, the humor of execution remain intact. I have a watercolor painting of a brilliant rooster, standing on big yellow feet, flaunting his tail feathers of purple and gold.

Since Walter Anderson's death in 1965, exhibitions of his work have travelled to many cities, and books of his "logs" and art continue to appear.

So these were the poles, the Bay and old hotel, speaking of a little understood past, and the Shearwater Pottery, alive with the present mystery of art continuing its course.

But there was also the inner private mystery of my own—the romance that went wrong, the relationship that could not survive. It's in life, not in literature, that we learn about irony. Before I left the coast in the spring of 1952, I made a bonfire of love letters in the yard behind my apartment in Pass Christian, and found the smoke useful for standing in to keep off the mosquitoes, which were especially hungry back there.

The second irony I must mention is bolder, bigger, and not to be survived. Many years later, that very spot where I caught my breath to see the Gulf in all its expanse and glory, found itself in the target eye of a destruction so complete the coast as we knew it could never be restored. Its name was Hurricane Camille.

Other hurricanes, memorable ones, had struck the area. One in 1947 burst the sea wall to bits; it was replaced by a man-made beach of white sand. Betsy, in 1965, swept the beach away; it was built up again. But to Camille, all such efforts might have been sand castles left by a child. It was repeated too often to be false that here was the most powerful hurricane ever to strike the continent, none stronger to be found in any record or in human memory.

I was living in 1969 in Montreal, but I saw more than enough of it on tv. I saw the few cars that crept through a world that was falling, not vertically down, but bursting apart horizontally, trees, buildings and telephone poles fighting like wild cats through the haze of wind and water to remain, slowly losing a nightlong battle. I saw evacuation moving massively along the highways north, heard stations fading from the air, until all communication like threads snipped one by one, was cut. I was left in the distant northern dark, to dream of other horrors still—my favorite old mansions crashing to flinders, little piers lifted from their pilings to coil like whips in the storm's fury, giant oaks with their roots nakedly exposed. But whatever I could imagine would still be less than the actual disasters of August 17, 1969.

Further shocks awaited when I returned to the area in the summer of 1970 to do a reading at Gulf Park, a junior college whose solid concrete buildings had survived the holocaust. I flew to New Orleans and rode to Gulfport on the bus. As we approached the coast through the marshy land east of New Orleans, I heard a woman talking behind me to someone she was sitting by. She had had to wait out the hurricane in Biloxi, at the hospital bedside of her father, who was too ill to be moved. "It was something more than natural," she kept repeating. "It was like one of them bomb experiments done got loose. It was just a lot more awful than anything natural could be." The tremor in her voice made me think that it had come that night and would not leave her.

Not that I could blame her. The bus reached Bay St. Louis and crossed the bridge. Here to the right was open water, calm and innocent, but to the left everything had changed. The shoreline and the road were at least twenty yards higher than before, and everything that had stood to the right of the road had vanished. A wonderful alley of oaks, a cool tunnel of bearded moss, was simply gone, as were the noble white houses just beyond them, and all their gardens. Double staircases, high verandahs like a dream of long summer afternoons, tall white-painted fences with wrought-iron gates, all were gone. Only walkways remained.

Just back of the bare re-routed beach drive, I later saw whole groves of pine trees reduced to blackened stumps as though burnt-over land. I was told that sand driven by winds that had reached 200 miles an hour (and probably much more: instruments at the time could go no higher), had blackened whatever it struck. How far back did the monster range, how far along the coast had it foraged? Sickened by the loss I saw, I didn't want to hear any more statistics. The real message was written already in the ragged shoreline, the disappearance of the little Pass Christian Yacht Club with brave flags and trim marina, the few stricken and displaced houses which had somehow got through. This place was finished. "Gone with the wind," is waiting to be wryly said here. It may be in order to observe with Camille, with her demure name like a Southern belle, did a better job than Sherman.

I knew I must write about all this some day. I had already done a number of stories—most of them in these pages—about various points along the Gulf or in the Caribbean. The writer A. J. Leibling, who loved the area, insisted that the Caribbean was this hemisphere's Mediterranean Sea. I agree. Its ways of life, its mystery, belong to the sea and create life styles and outlooks which are totally, rhythmically different from what we think of as our own "normal" ways of living.

But beyond all that, it was the hurricane itself, its wild force and aftermath, that stayed with me and finally grew into the novel *The Salt Line*, which I was many years in writing. I took a number of trips to the coast, lingering for weeks at the time. I heard hundreds of stories from people I knew who lived there. I read through innumerable accounts in the all new library in Gulfport. I even went out once more to Ship Island. The lighthouse was gone, no victim of Camille, which she had somehow gallantly weathered, but burnt down, I was told, by some boys on a lark. The island itself had been split in two parts by the storm. Now land which had offered the first harbor the French explorers had found, the scene of historic wartime events, decades of Sunday School picnics, and countless romantic afternoons, was two diminished little islands with the sea flowing between.

Back at Pass Christian the little Gothic-style white painted Episcopal church in its grove of oaks was gone— the rector, I learned, had seen his wife and child drowned in the tidal wave, while he held to the front steps and reached out vainly to bring them in.

But worse than all this was to see what was now moving into this lost world. Condos and shopping centers, Holiday Inns and Howard Johnsons and Best Westerns, Wendy's and Waffle Houses. A few new houses with no friendly groves to nestle in.

Ocean Springs, however, I found to my delight, was little touched. Biloxi had a charming new square. There were little theatres springing up, the old Magnolia Hotel was a showplace gallery for colorful coastal painting, and some new shops showed sensitivity to the locale. Best of all, the Shearwater Pottery had been spared. It was still to be reached by its shaggy winding road, and there I discovered what others had found after the death of Walter Anderson. A hidden treasure was in a small cottage adjacent to the main house and the pottery, where he had lived in later years quite alone, his place of refuge.

This singular man had died soon after sitting through Hurricane Betsy in 1965 out on Horn Island. He had gone out on purpose to get as close as possible to the invader. It is well known that Horn Island, like the cottage, was his special province. He had rowed out to it often, stayed there for weeks at the time, kept a journal about his experiences and, of course, painted and drew its creatures, plants, flowers, sand and sea. The hurricane to him must have been one more visiting live thing. He died soon after the experience of it, though not before rejoicing in his logs:

> Never has there been a hurricane more respectable, provided with all the portents, predictions, omens, etc., etc. The awful sunrise—no one could fail to take a warning from it—the hovering black spirit bird (man o'war)—only one—(*comme il faut*) . . . .

In the cottage (now forbidden to visitors without special permission), I saw the room he had painted entirely in murals, the walls speaking everywhere in brilliant colors, of his vision of the coast, its myth and its reality. The book that reproduces these astonishing works is called *A Painter's Psalm*. I know of no greater work anywhere in this country—we may safely go to Europe for achievement to compare to it.

The character central to *The Salt Line*, Arnold Carrington, also has a vision of the coast. Regretting Camille's destruction, he tries to restore. Many of his feelings are echoes of my own:

> . . . the old pre-hurricane Coast: shrimp boats and ancient oaks, camellias in bloom, flags flying from the old white lighthouse, moonlight on the Sound, softly blowing curtains of Spanish moss . . . where to find this unity of house, shade, and sun . . . the brick walk,

the moss barely stirring to its familiar breeze of this hour, this peace and precious past. . . .

No, it can never return, but one thing does remain intact—the air and light.

Lafcadio Hearn: This strange gulf air "compels awe— something vital, something holy, something pantheistic."

The novelist John William DeForrest spoke of the "atmospheric magic" of the Gulf.

The architect Louis Sullivan declaimed on the "luxury of peace within the velvety carressing air."

If only that Interstate No. 10 had not come so close! These great speedways pull like a current; they warp whatever lies nearby.

I read in a recent review of some of my own books, that I set *The Salt Line* on the Gulf Coast, better known as the "redneck Riviera." I was thunderstruck. Was not even enough left standing to correct this coarse ignorance of the past? Was this the post-hurricane phrase that could actually be thought to apply?

I hope I never hear anyone say it. I will wish curses down upon him. He, too, shall one day be in a hurricane's target eye.

—ELIZABETH SPENCER

ON THE GULF

Mary Dee went out in the heat in the early afternoon and began to swing. Back and forth, back and forth, sitting with her skirt around her, flying open and shut. It was something to do.

Semmes, their old colored woman, came out and said, "Don't swing so high, Dee-dee. It worries your mama."

"She's on the other side," said Mary Dee, swooping past.

There was a daytime moon. When she went her highest, her tennis shoes rested on it.

"Them folks coming from N'Orlens. You know how your mama is about company."

"Wears her out," said Mary Dee, and getting tired, her hair damp and hot, she let the cat die. It died slow as anything, then she was scarcely moving over the bare place in the grass where you pushed, and then she turned around until the ropes wound tightly around each other, going higher and higher. She let herself go, spinning. She did that three times.

"Your head swimming, I bet," said Semmes. She was sitting down now, a little way off, in a lawn chair.

"Whyn't you go to the pool?" Semmes asked.

"It's too late. Time I get there."

"Ain't no more than three-thirty."

"Ain't you got to cook?"

"Certainly I do. Got to start in."

"Who's coming?" Mary Dee asked, the first she'd thought to wonder. At the table when there was company she sat and said, "Yes, ma'am," and "No, ma'am"; her mother liked it that way.

"Them Meades," said Semmes. "Comes every summer. Eats like horses."

"It's cool out here; over there it's hot," Mary Dee said.

"Ain't that entirely. They counts on my dinner, Dee-dee." She looked toward the house. It was two-story, red brick, old, with a big side yard where they were. It was afternoon-still. Way up in the live oak, even the Spanish moss looked as sound asleep at that hour as a dog would be. "Any minute now, Miss Annie going to get out of that bed and start straightening up."

"When I grow up I'm not going to worry any." Mary Dee started spinning the other way.

"One time them Meades come and got into rain crossing the Pearl. Rain like brickbats; hail big as eggs. I'd a-turnt back, been me. No, sir! Car dented all over the roof with hail. Hail that big around. Chunks big enough to put in the highballs, which they did. Frozen solid."

Mary Dee stopped. "How'd they get it?"

"It skips, don't you know. Goes bouncing along. Put their hand out the car window and caught it. That's how. Blamming on the roof of the car. Them Meades inside, scared and laughing both. I ain't so struck on them Meades."

"Mama's not either. I heard her say so. Twice. 'I just can't stand them another year.' That's what she said."

"They keep on coming," said Semmes. "It's got to be regular."

"What you going to have?"

"Crawfish bisque, stuffed hen, pickled peaches, biscuits, cauliflower, beets, tomatoes, rice and beans on the side, strawberry chill with macaroons. Chicory."

"Same as ever," said Mary Dee.

"Between here and Florida, ain't no cook good as me," said Semmes.

"And we got you," said Mary Dee, complacently, repeating what she'd heard.

"Got to take me home, though," Semmes gloated. "Got to go get me. Even if I move a hundred miles. I ain't walking nowhere. Not before I die."

"When you die? Where you think you can walk to when you die?"

"Lord knows," said Semmes. "He tell me, chile."

"I'm eight years old," said Mary Dee, not knowing exactly what she meant, and ran into the house.

Semmes scratched in her ear with a straw, and presently, smoothing out her dress, she got up and walked over to the fish pond. She turned one or two of the lawn chairs straight on the paving around the water, brushing them free of twigs and droppings. Gulls were the worst. Sometimes, when stiff weather came on, rain hanging in dark splotches way out on the gulf, the gulls sailed in to refugee. Once they ate the goldfish. The glass-top table needed polishing. That was Miss Annie's job. Mister Lawrence could dip trash from the pool. The car would ease in through the gate. Soon they would all be out here, getting drunk and acting crazy about one another, with Dee-dee in a big prissy sash and white socks, passing canapes. A goldfish, biggest in the pool, came above the surface and looked Semmes in the eye.

Semmes had a familiar spirit she often spoke with, something she'd got many years ago, at just about Mary Dee's age. She'd been to the nuns' school and nothing she had learned there discouraged her from having this spirit around, though in one way or other, what with so many things happening, wars and elections and everything, times different, she never talked about it. Every now and then she picked up a piece of colored glass, a sort of blue glass, apt to be iridescent, some shells, some little rock, and just going along, whenever she took a notion, she threw these things aside, and maybe the spirit got them. Did it eat them? How would she know what it did?

"Organdy's scratchy," said Mary Dee, upstairs and complaining. "It's a beautiful dress," said her mother. "Even Daddy noticed."

"I wore it Sunday."

"Semmes can press it. Just take it in the kitchen, hang it on the chair. I haven't got time."

"Mama, why do we have to have the Meades?"

Her mother, filing her nails, fresh from her bath, sitting in a loose cotton robe and slippers, legs crossed, eyes lowered, flashed her a look and smiled. "Don't you say that in front of them, monkey."

"But why do we?"

"They brag on things out here. We went to their open house once, after the Sugar Bowl. They have this lovely old house with original floorboards a yard wide. Then they call up and say Come to Antoine's, but we never can." She threw the file aside. "I don't know. Daddy says that too. I just don't know. I declare I don't."

"So much to *do*," said Mary Dee, who did not have to do anything but march into the kitchen with her dress. She sat in the chaise longue and let it comfortably engulf her. She looked out at the sky. From here you could see the water. Two gulls were sailing so far up they looked carefully shaped and thin, like the scalloped edges of a pillow case. They passed across the daytime moon. "First it's over yonder, now it's over here," said Mary Dee.

"What is, precious?"

"The moon."

"Don't bite your nails," said her mother.

"'A girl is known,'" said Mary Dee, quoting—she had felt guilt for a moment, then she joked it away—"'by her hands, her skin, her carriage, and her hair. We cannot all be beautiful.'"

"You're getting too smart," said her mother. "Who's going to tell you things if I don't? Someday you'll be glad to know all that."

"Have the Meades got any children?"

"Just that brother that always comes."

"He caught the hail, I bet," said Mary Dee.

"That was the silliest thing," said her mother. "They should have gone straight back. Right into that black cloud."

"Daddy said Come hell or high water."

"Daddy said that but you ought not to."

A wonderful odor, spicy and rich, began to come up from below. They both looked toward the direction of it, as though it could not only be seen but could look back.

"That bisque," her mother murmured, biting her lip with hunger and pride, a combination not so rare in that household.

Mary Dee jumped up suddenly. She had not gone swimming at the pool that day, but the feeling of swimming came strongly over her, out of habit, so she ran and dived straight into the bed, kicking her brown legs and flailing her arms until exhausted.

"Them old Meades." Now she was mimicking Semmes. "I wish they's gone already."

Her mother shot her a glance, even sharper than before. "Don't you know better than to carry on like that?

What are you trying to grow up to be? That's what I'd like to know! Stop listening to us! Stop hearing anything we say!"

THE LEGACY

In the stillness, from three blocks over, Dottie Almond could hear a big diesel truck out on the highway, climbing the grade up to the stoplight, stopping, shifting gears and passing on.

She went and brushed her hair that was whiter than pull candy and rubbed a little dime store lipstick on her mouth. In the bathroom window, her cousin Tandy's big white buckskin shoes all but covered the sill. They were outlined with swirling perforated leather strips, toe and heel and nest for laces, and had been placed there to dry. When he got back from Memphis, he would probably be going out on a date or out on the highway someplace or "just out," which was what he said when you never knew. He had never asked Dottie anywhere, never told her anything, never talked to her once. She kept notes on him from such things as cleaned up shoes.

She had heard them—Aunt Hazel and Tandy—out in the living room the night she came. They had thought she was asleep, she had been so dead tired when she'd gone to bed.

"One more mouth to feed, huh?" Tandy said. Whatever he said, it was always as if he were telling jokes, the subject of this present joke being what his mother had got into about Dottie.

"You don't have to look at it that way," Aunt Hazel said. "She had to be somewhere."

"Just keep her out of my things. She gets in my things, she's going to know it."

"Try and be nice to her."

"Not paying us a cent."

"Well, I know, but try your best. Be nice to her."

"Oh, I'll be nice to her." The tone went up; it was an unpromising voice, off center. If it made a promise, the promise might be its opposite because a word had got twisted around. "I'll be nice to her, all right."

Dottie's father worked in Birmingham and did not make much money. She'd had to go somewhere, which was why Aunt Hazel had taken her in. There was also a Great Aunt Maggie Lee Asquith, who (she had said) would have done the same and that she ought to, but she was too old, all alone in a big house in the middle of a Delta "place." A young girl like that—gul, she called it—a young gul like that ought to have young people around. Aunt Hazel and Tandy lived in a town with young people in it. They were the ones to take her in.

"How long you been with Miss Hazel?" The speaker was a Mr. Avery Donelson, to whose law office Dottie had just been summoned.

"About a year."

Hanging down from the straight chair one foot couldn't quite touch the floor. She crossed her legs, in order to resemble any other girl, though the man at the desk gave no sign of noticing. She had heard her father once say that Mr. Avery Donelson was a high class fellow.

"Your family has a high mortality rate," he remarked, and seemed almost prepared to be amused about it.

Dottie didn't laugh. Death to her had nothing to do with anybody except her mother (who had held her hand when she hurt from polio and who was right there, everything they did to her. "When you hurt, I hurt, baby. Just think about that. Only I hurt twice as bad." Nobody else who had died—or lived either—had ever said that.) However, Aunt Hazel's husband Uncle Jack had died of a stroke uptown one hot day three years ago, and Aunt Maggie Lee had gone quick, from cancer, just last spring. Dorothy hadn't attended the funeral. Her daddy wouldn't let her. He had come over from Birmingham to stay with her while Aunt Hazel went. Aunt Maggie Lee was her mother's side of the family. "You go on, Hazel," Daddy said. "My little ole sugar's not going to any more ole funerals." He had taken her out to eat in a restaurant and then, as they couldn't find anything to talk about, he took her to the picture show. The show was sad so she got to cry in it. What she was thinking about was her mother's funeral. Maybe he had known that because he held her hand. When they got home Aunt Hazel and Tandy had got back from the Delta where Aunt Maggie Lee's funeral was held that afternoon, and Daddy gave Dottie a lot of wet smacking kisses and called her his little ole honey bun, and went off back to Birmingham, late as it was. She thought that Aunt Hazel made him nervous. "He's always got business somewhere," was what Aunt Hazel said. . . .

"I knew your Aunt Miss Maggie Lee pretty well," Mr. Avery Donelson said. "She was quite a stepper." He seemed to be enjoying himself.

"What's a stepper?" Dottie asked. So far she hadn't smiled; feeling herself observed, she kept her blue eyes steady, thought of her skin which was darker than her taffy-white hair.

"She was a fine lady," he said. "Knew how to dress, how to talk. Kept a good house, set a good table. Lived in good circumstances. Husband was a planter. Left her well-fixed."

Dottie had herself known Aunt Maggie Lee. She and her mother had gone once or twice to visit her and stayed overnight, in the Delta, a long way from Birmingham. Mother was a little nervous and hoped Dottie and she were behaving all right, especially at the table. Aunt Maggie Lee sat up straight in graceful antique chairs; yet on the second day she lay down on a sofa for a while. ("Maggie Lee's tired," Mother said to someone when they returned. "I think something's wrong.") She had a kind of cosmetics Dottie had never seen in stores and her bathrooms were rosy, her house soft with rugs and dim lights because the Delta in the summer was full of glare; air conditioning was essential and curtains had to stay drawn. With her mother out of the room, Aunt Maggie Lee questioned Dottie extensively on a number of subjects. "Do you have a hobby?" she asked. "I collect things," Dottie said. "What, for instance?" "Bird cards from Arm and Hammer soda boxes, for one thing." "What else?" "Pencils, all different colors." When she was sick, for some reason, everybody started giving her boxes of pencils. She had all colors now. If she got one the same color as another she would go out and exchange it for a color she didn't have. "Birds are of some interest," said Aunt Maggie Lee. "But pencils. . . ."

"She kept up with you," Mr. Avery Donelson went on. "She knew about your making good grades in school. She thought you must have a little bit of what it took. I wanted to see you alone because of what she did for you. She made a special bequest for you before she died."

"Bequest?"

"A settlement . . . money . . . all yours. But—a secret."

Dottie was quaking again now; another one had known of her, thought and spoken of her, made her a secret and formal gift. It sounded like something God might do.

"You're not interested in how much?" Mr. Avery Donelson finally said.

"Five hundred dollars?" Then she blushed. Greed was what she knew she'd sounded like.

"How about ten thousand?"

"Ten thousand? What? Pennies?" A wise crack was not the right thing. She had just reached the conclusion it was all a big joke.

"Dollars, young lady. And if you don't want 'em, there's plenty that will."

"I didn't mean that. It seemed like—It was a surprise, that's all."

"Don't you like surprises?"

"It was a big surprise."

"You sing in school, I hear."

So he knew that, too. Her contralto voice had a rich thrill in it when she let go with a song. She and everybody else had found out about this by accident, trying out songs. They all liked to hear her, even the teachers, and they got her to sing at school programs sometimes. There would be dances, too, to sing at, but she wouldn't go to them. If you were crippled it was better not to go. But on rainy days she could hold the student body down in the auditorium at recess, singing almost anything anybody wanted to play for her. Her mother had never known she could sing, not like that.

"What do you want to be?" Mr. Avery Donelson pressed her. "That's a good sum of money, you know. Set up in trust until you turned eighteen, it could see you some of the way through college. Your Aunt Hazel wouldn't be able to afford to send you to college."

"Tandy doesn't like it because I live there free of charge," said Dottie. "He thinks I ought to pay. Maybe Aunt Hazel would think it, too, if she knew I could."

"Then don't mention it," he said at once. "You don't have to. We can say it's in trust for you, just for college."

"But it's not, is it?"

"She wanted you to decide, that's all. Me to adminis-trate, advise. You to decide."

Through slats in the venetian blinds Dottie could see the town water tank, painted silver, the tops of the trees, see the still, hot, morning sky. The window air conditioner purred. Mr. Avery Donelson had brown and white hori-zontally striped curtains, a rug, a desk, some black leather chairs. His secretary was outside and the door was closed. He would never call a daughter "little ole honey bun," and if he took her to dinner he would know what to talk about. He had known Aunt Maggie Lee who was a stepper like himself and who had picked Dottie out for possible entry into a world different from Aunt Hazel's.

But did she *have* to be what they had decided, what-ever it was? They had taken her consent for granted. She was dazed.

"I got to think it over, don't I?"

The carpet took her halting walk. The man at the desk—grey, unmoving, well-suited but casually rumpled— had stopped smiling, sat watching instead, his attention all finally upon her. He rose to open the door. She was a small girl, came hardly to his top vest button.

"It's in the bank for you. I'm supposed to do anything you say, young lady." He pressed her hand.

Then she was through the office, down the stairs and on the hot sidewalk that led back to Aunt Hazel's, hot and chill together in the scald of the sun, a jerky progress through the dazzle.

All that money poured out on me, *me*, ME! She almost struck herself on the forehead. Transparent as a locust's wing the frail self within tried to stir, to take up whatever was meant by it; since it was recognized, it ought to emerge and fly. But all it was was Dorothy Almond, plodding back toward her few small treasures and necessities, toward pencils and bird cards no two the same, her four or five cotton dresses, her slacks and blouses, her new white sandals.

When she came in the front door the phone was ringing. "I called you twice," said Aunt Hazel, on the other end.

"I was in the bathtub."

"You must have stayed till you shrivelled. I have to work through dinner. Just fix yourself something."

"Yessum."

"Did the paper ever come?"

"Yessum."

"Did Tandy call?"

"No'm. I don't guess he did."

"I don't reckon so. I'll see you this evening, honey."

Dottie went and looked to see if the big white male shoes were still on the bathroom window sill. They were. There was nowhere else they could have gone. Men's shoes, white, heavy, secretive, knowledgeable—they derided her as much after as before Mr. Avery Donelson's call had smashed into her silence. All else had changed and diminished; they were the same. What did she expect? She had heard of a distant cousin who had stuck his finger up an empty socket to see whether, since the bulb would not work, the lamp was broken. It wasn't. Was it a shock she had expected when she put her hand out and ran her fingers over those shoes, heel to vamp to toe? Shoes like these, only brown, were now treading pavement in Memphis, Tennessee, with Tandy in them. He was going to know the minute he looked that something had happened to her, and he would find out what it was, right away. Now she was scared. A call to life was one thing, but getting the first breath kicked straight out of you—It would happen if she wasn't careful. She called up Avery Donelson.

"You said I could have anything, anytime."

"That's right."

"Can I have five hundred dollars, then?"

"Certainly."

"Can I get it at two o'clock?"

"That's possible."

"Will you put all the rest where nobody can get it, just tell them if they ask you that five hundred dollars was all there was, that was all?"

A hesitance. "If you say so."

She had climbed his answers like stairsteps, one by one; they had taken her higher and higher, to the very top, and at that top—like saying "Walk!" the way they had in the hospital and she had held her breath and walked, the leg feeling liquid at first and numb, then thin as a toothpick but holding—so at this final moment in what was happening now, she had to jump, which was more than walk; and the jump was trust.

"Do you promise?" She clutched the receiver. Her eyes were squinched up tight.

"I promise." She was held, so far, unfailing.

The bus to Birmingham had left, as Dottie had known it would from visiting her father, at two-thirty. She was on it. Near a window, bolt upright with five hundred dollars—less the price of the ticket—in her purse, she was drawn forward above the landscape like a pulled-out string. In the Birmingham bus station, she dialed Daddy on the pay telephone, holding her finger on his number in the book. A woman's voice answered "Hell-o?" too loud. Dottie asked for Mr. Almond, then added, for some reason, "I'm his daughter," but the woman said she had the wrong number. She tried again, but though she let the phone ring six times, nobody answered it. Maybe he was still at work. She tried Southern Railway, where he had his office, but only got the ticket counter, and when she tried to explain, they couldn't hear her, there was such a lot of noise at the other end, and then she was out of change. She walked out into the station, which smelled of frying hamburgers, still remembering the woman's voice on the phone. She attained to an enormous lack of conviction about things involved in finding Daddy, and seeing a bus with Miami on the front, she bought a ticket and climbed into it. On the bus, at intervals, she slept. Miami was not till the next day. When she got there, she didn't know what to do, so took another bus that said Key West. In Key West there was nothing to do either, but it was the end. Dottie went to a motel of separate cabins in a shady park full of plants, rented one, and fell asleep.

It was the end of running; that she knew. Like a small planet, she had set.

Another day, freshly risen, she sat in a newly bought bathing suit on a sandy beach with one leg tucked under her, looking out at the sea. There were huge clouds above her, all the same color as her hair, which made them seem more personal than they might have been to brunettes or redheads.

There was a boy circling round, a man, really, though younger than Tandy and certainly better to look at. He was all bronze and gold, like a large, well-formed wasp, she thought, as he had the same copper hair on his head, chest, arms and legs. And his drift—the way he spoke to her, looked at her—was something like that of a wasp which might or might not be thinking favorably of you. He asked her if she wanted to swim, and she told him no.

"You're getting sunburned," he said.

"I'm all right," she said.

"Where you staying?"

"The Hibiscus."

"Walk you home?"

She shook her head, gazing up at the clouds. But he was right. She was getting sunburned. She wished he'd go. She wished he'd leave her alone. Then he did.

Dottie had told him the truth about the Hibiscus because she had done nothing lately but tell lies. The first night away, for instance, at a bus stop, she had phoned Aunt Hazel so Aunt Hazel wouldn't call out the F.B.I., or the highway patrol, or whatever you called out, to look for her. She had said:

"Aunt Hazel, I hope you found the letter I left."

What followed was such a volley of words that Dottie felt sorry for Aunt Hazel, who when she got to worrying about things there was no stopping her. "Let me tell you something, honey. It's just ridiculous for you to go off like that. If Maggie Lee had known you'd be spending all her money at the beach, she never would have left you a dime, let alone five hundred dollars. But there you are throwing it away, *five hundred dollars*, and with any number of things you really need, and I can't think of why anybody would be that inconsiderate, as good as Tandy and I have been to you. Why didn't you at least go see your daddy in Birmingham?"

"I tried to call him, but he wasn't there."

"You ain't with anybody?"

"No'm."

"Well, you'd just better mind out," Aunt Hazel said. And when Dottie didn't answer she said, "You'll phone me every night until you get home? I'm going to worry about you every single night."

Dottie stayed in the shady little cabin she had rented at Hibiscus Cottages All Conveniences Pool TV. You reached the cabins through winding paved paths bordered by plants and flowering shrubs, shaded by palms. It was a pretty place, and not many people were there. Not that many people came to Key West in the summer, so they said. If you swam in the pool, the water felt like you could just as well take a bath in it. She read some movie magazines, then a paperback mystery book, then made a ham sandwich and ate it, ate a tomato whole with salt, ate some coconut marshmallow cookies, some pink, some white, and drank a glass of milk. Then she lay down and looked at TV and fell asleep with the air conditioner purring. At four o'clock she went walking. It was still hot all over town, hot as an oven, but the clouds had got bigger and from somewhere off she heard a tumble of thunder.

At the end of a street, she could look at the gulf, and way out there she saw the big clouds piled higher than ever before, the silver color darkening from the top downward. She turned her back on them and walked into town, past houses with plants round them, oleanders, a stubby sort of grass, pale faded green or artificial funeral-parlor bright green, not like the grass up home, and always palms, some bent and low as plants, some real tree-size. The trees she liked the best were—she'd been told by an old lady on the bus coming down—emperor palms. The trunks of the palms were round, swelled out at mid-height but narrow at top and bottom, and looked to be made of stone, with a bunch of thick palm fronds coming out of the top, as though stuck in a too-tall vase. They were pretty trees, Dottie decided, and when the afternoon rain hit Key West and she had no idea which way to go to get back, she went and sat under one of them, at the corner of somebody's property. It was probably the most dangerous place to be, as the tree was high and would attract a lightning bolt possibly, but its top was waving in such an impressive way she thought she'd rather be here than elsewhere. She crouched there as the rain fell in ropes. Soon she was soaked to the skin.

When the sun burst out again she started returning by trial and error and so came into the Hibiscus from the back, before she knew it. Standing in the garden, also wet, wearing beige cotton trousers, a tee-shirt and a dripping slicker was the copper-haired boy she had met at the beach. She ran right into him and then seeing it wasn't just a coincidence, that he was coming toward her, she turned around and started off through the paths. He had to run and catch her arm. She stopped, head down and shuddering, like she'd seen wild animals do in the country the minute some boy would get his hands on them. She drooped like that and didn't look.

"What'd you come for?" she said.

"You're not from around here, are you?"

She shook her head.

"What are you limping about?" he said.

"Something fell on me."

The boy looked around at the maze of paths, the village of cottages spotted out amongst the dripping foliage. "Where's yours?"

"Number ten."

He was half-holding her up but before he got to the door, he thought it simpler to carry her, and so did. "Give me your key." She took out the key but, being let down, stood holding herself upright by the door, downcast, still, and tremulous. "Nothing really fell on me," she said.

"But you're hurt, obviously."

"I'm crippled."

"Is that why you wouldn't go swimming?"

"Please," she said.

She felt his large warm hand drop from her arm. "Okay." He drew back, looking at her with a different air altogether. Was she glad or not? She didn't know. She thought she must have looked terrible after the rain. Like a drowned white rat, she thought, closing the door on him, leaning against it.

She was still hearing his voice and not answering it. New feeling—fresh, sharp, hurting—had sprung up as though branches of her blood had turned into vines which were determined all by themselves to flourish in her. It was what she thought it would never do any good to look for. She fell face down across the bed. She might have known, but hadn't. She could have said that in addition to being lame, her mother had died, and that the lawyer Mr. Avery Donelson had sent for her, and that her Aunt Miss Maggie Lee Asquith, well-known in the Delta, had left her a legacy of $10,000, a part of which, in the opinion of Aunt Hazel, she was now throwing away in Florida. She was somebody picked out. Being lame *in itself* was being picked out. But he wouldn't see any of that. He wasn't from where she was. All that travelled with her was a short leg.

And her white hair, whiter than taffy, born white, said the streak of sun coming through the one slat of blind which had got twisted.

Late in the afternoon, her hair brushed and combed, face washed, she walked down the main street of Key West, past the big square hotel. She was looking for somewhere to eat and went past a big open bar where a sign said Ernest Hemingway used to sit and drink. Among palms, and near a large spreading tree with red flowers, she saw a brick-red-painted, barn-like building whose sign, also outside, said it was a playhouse. Another sign, of hastily lettered green on white cardboard, said that tryouts for a play were being held. Dottie hobbled to the door and found it open. She went through an empty foyer plastered with posters, and through a second large heavy door into an auditorium with a stage before it and rows of folding chairs, some disarranged, some open and placed in regular lines, others closed and propped against the walls.

A tall dark woman like the still statue of a goddess, wearing a crumpled linen dress and leather sandals, was standing near the center of the stage, which was lighted artificially, with a large bound sheaf of pages in her hand, open half the way through, back folded on itself. Her hands were long, and tanned, and aware of themselves, her whole self was aware and nurtured, her black hair tumbled the way she wanted it to around her face. She was pointing out to three or four others on the stage with her, younger than she, what they ought to do, what *she* thought they ought to do, how this, how that. She turned, walked away, leaned back against a table and picked up a half-smoked cigarette from an ashtray, inhaling, pluming smoke; her body gave life to the clinging linen. At the lift of her fingers, the young actors, all about Dottie's age, holding smaller books, began to read aloud. Dottie hated the large woman of authority in linen and sandals . . . she was afraid of her by instinct. She turned to go away, but was called to.

"Hey, blondie!"

Obedient, not showing what she felt, she turned back and limped forward, down between the raggedly arranged chairs. The woman had come to the footlights, and as Dottie approached, the former went down on one knee, as though kneeling by the edge of a pool to retrieve something. She did it like poetry. Dottie's face was a mask, looking up at her.

"You want to try out? What can you do?"

"Sing," said Dottie.

"Sing what?"

The boys were talking now, over the footlights, the words falling toward her lifted face: "Rock?" "Revival?" "Country Western?"

"Just sing," Dottie said. "Popular mostly."

"There's all kinds of popular," one of the boys said. "But, hey—stick around. We expected more people. . . . Take a script."

"Take mine," another boy said.

"You know this play? It's *Picnic.* There's a song in it somewhere, at least I think there is."

"Or we'll put one in," somebody said, and another: "She looks like Kim Novak."

"I'm crippled," Dottie said, right out. "I can sing, that's all."

There was a quick silence, like a whole orchestra gone dead. Then they reached their arms down and pulled her up over the footlights, out of the dark and onto the bright stage. She hobbled over to the piano and a girl about her age came and sat down to play for her. She sang one of the songs she liked, and they clapped, saying with astonished voices how wonderful she was, and she knew it, too.

She had bought herself a little cap, like a sailor's cap, at an open air shop along the way where things were all displayed, and when she sang her song she held this in her small hands and knew it made a good effect. When they shot a spotlight on her face she didn't mind a bit. A sissy boy at school used to turn his spotlight on her: she was used to it. Her face and voice went floating away from her legs, off from the part they could forget while she sang. She heard them applaud again and she heard what they said and then she sang again and told them that was all.

The light switched off. The large woman seemed to her to have gone completely, but this was not so; she had gone out of the circle of light to sit on the edge of a table.

Then they were leaving. Dottie was moving with them, or they with her, as she was not going with them in spirit, but only moving alone though among them, through the disarray of chairs in the big dusky barn-like room, and feeling not so far from home, for it resembled the high school auditorium where she had held many more people for an even longer time. She heard them speaking to her but was not answering; and then the daylight struck through the second door they opened, not glaring as when she had entered, but softened by evening. There was a car freshly pulled up behind the yellow Pontiac which had been parked there when Dottie went in, and the boy was in it, the one from the beach and the storm, just getting out when he saw them come through the door. She saw him get out, turning as he closed the door the way she had seen good basketball players turn without seeming to move at all, the way dancers follow each other. He was there for them, she knew at once: his approach said so. And she knew too why she had been afraid of the dark woman.

Dottie left the crowd and walked across the street.

"Hi." The boy was following her.

"Hi." She didn't stop walking.

"You're in the play?"

"Ask them," she said and kept limping on.

The pool was a quiet rectangle with no one swimming in it, and the people who circled, stood, wound, and twined and drank and talked with one another, moved like columns, slowly revolving and changing place, one to another, in long dresses, in white jackets, reflecting in the water. The house was built around this open area, with a balustrade above in white painted wood such as Dottie thought she'd seen in pictures or paintings. There were brick-colored urns of geraniums and a long twining plant with purplish blue blooms as if a head of hair had decked itself that way, and there were others, yellow and pink and white. No one walked on the balustrades, or climbed the stairs. They turned, columnar and decorous, with muted voices, around the still pool. They sipped from glasses that sparkled with amber whisky or white gin on crystal ice.

"No, thank you," said Dottie. "Just some water," she said.

She refused not from righteousness or inexperience but simply because she was drunk already, having earlier ordered three martinis in a restaurant somewhere near the Hibiscus. Later, she'd been found wandering around the old Spanish fort, jumping off and on the parapet, pretending nothing was the matter with her while all sorts of wild ideas somersaulted through her head—been found by the copper-haired boy and another, his friend.

In the friend's car, all of Key West had looped and dived around her like a dolphin. If you got drunk, how long did you have to stay drunk? She was wondering this when the friend stopped before a Spanish-type house and once inside began pulling evening skirts out of a closet.

"Try any one you want."

"You got a sister?" Dottie said.

"She's not here. Besides, she wouldn't mind. She swaps clothes all the time," he said with a laugh to the boy Dottie knew, the copper-haired boy. Johnny was his name.

The phone rang and Johnny's friend went to answer it. Johnny threw his arms around Dottie and tumbled her back on the bed. She lay there a little while with his arms around her. Then they heard the other boy coming back and she got up to try the skirts on. In the long skirt she felt un-crippled. She moved her built-up sandal in a different way, just like her hips were swaying. Pretty, pretty, she thought, looking in the mirror. I can be like magic.

Then they drove to another house, the big one with the drive. There Dottie saw the dark woman whom in linen she had hated, only she was columnar now, standing by the still pool in a bold drop of yellow with great white wings or fronds and a white binding against the tan of her bare arms and her hair in rich careless coils.

"They tell me you sing, young lady."

The speaker was a man, the host here, with dark thinning hair combed straight back. He smiled at Dottie and showed teeth that looked false.

"Yes, sir," she said.

He asked her where she'd come from, where she went to school, where she wanted to go to college. She must have been saying things back.

"Can you sing for us?" he said. "Some time this evening, I mean."

"I'm sorry."

"Oh, you must," he said.

"I got drunk," Dottie said.

The beautiful dark head above the bare brown back showed it had heard her and was turning. The carefully painted mask hung perfectly. Dottie wanted to be with people who wouldn't notice her too much. Nobody would have cared what she said except the dark woman, who was, of course, her enemy, and said nothing.

Dottie started climbing the flight of stairs. A Cuban-looking man in a white jacket had said she would find the bathroom up there. In passing she saw that a pottery urn filled with bloom was just above the head of the hostess, the dark woman, Pam, the enemy who did not want her to live. Dottie placed her hands, one on either side of the urn, and gazed, calculating, as one might along the barrel of a cousin's BB gun. She drank up the possibility of the action as she might another martini. This was what she needed to do, but couldn't. A door opened off in the shadowy passageway behind her, and she turned, surprised, unable to see anyone.

Later, coming out of the bathroom, she thought about the urn again but in a distant way. Johnny met her at the foot of the stairs with a banana daiquiri and somebody from above screamed, "Watch out!" They all looked up. An old woman with too-bright blond hair, too scarlet a mouth, was clutching at that same terra cotta urn, and everyone leaped aside as it swung, tottered, slipped past her painted nails and long pink chiffon handkerchief, smashing on the marble paving near the pool.

"Grandmother!"

The old woman, like a mad witch entered on a balcony during a play, leaned far out into the velvet air, calling, "I hit it by mistake! It just fell!"

To Dottie, who could not stop gazing above, it was like seeing herself sixty years from now, a grotesque double. Was it the old lady's door she had heard a while ago?

The Cuban, a servant it seemed, was picking up pieces of broken pottery which had scattered near Pam's skirt. Her husband, whom someone had jerked from the falling urn's path, mounted the stairs toward the old woman.

Conversation resumed. There was a drift toward a table of food. Someone remarked that half of Key West was there. Many of them were young, the age of Johnny, more or less.

I'll just sneak out, Dottie thought. I'll go home alone.

But she didn't go home alone, because Johnny reappeared to drive her, and not with the boy whose sister's skirt she wore, but Johnny alone and driving like the wind, racing out from Key West up the long highway that arrowed toward Marathon, then swirling off along back shell roads because he was high on something maybe liquor maybe not and talking a blue streak, and she was piecing it out the best she could, she Dottie Almond, to whom all of life was gradually reducing itself to one single problem: How To Stay Awake Another Minute. The day must have already been sixty-four hours long. She could hear him the way she might hear the sea rustling when asleep by it, or the way you'd hear prayers in church.

"Morrissey knew about it from the first and that I wasn't any killer, not a thief, and certainly that if I went too far that time, it was out of my own principles . . . how they got out of bounds. He had some good inside stuff about them, but when they put on the pressure, he was even able to swing a position elsewhere, it's how he got the big appointment . . . oh, Pam's money . . . you saw that house . . . where'd he be without it, nobody can say, only it's not so much money . . . just that he saw a way of getting me out, out of the country till it blew over . . . that was when Pam came looking. It was her idea . . . I'd swear to it anytime. . . ."

"Out of the country, where?" she mumbled, her mouth sticky inside from being sleepy.

"Think of anywhere. Mexico. Think of Canada."

She thought of Canada, but only saw polar bears. They had got back. He turned at the Hibiscus sign, and drifting in, stopped the car. Hundred-pound weights sat on her eyelids. "Look." He held his hands forward and turned up the dash light, then showed her his fingers, palm up. She could discern by the dim light what she'd seen before, the healed skin over finger ends which had been cut or burnt. She was still hearing the soft crush of shells beneath the tires, and then she felt the broken finger ends like pieces of screen printing her cheek and neck, then her mouth pressed and opened with his own. She remembered earlier how he'd pushed her down, knew her body had taken a note of it, like a secretary might write down a call to be made at a later moment which had now arrived. She was dead for sleep, opened the door herself to stumble out and find her cabin but instead was being carried, floating, skimming silently down along a smooth and swollen stream, face rising up above the surface, eyes closed, branches of oleander, vines of bougainvillea, hibiscus like trumpets, crisp and red.

She woke with sun coming in through the slant blinds, the long borrowed skirt crumpled on a chair, herself a trampled field with a game over, the score standing.

She lay there till she got hungry. No one came in the door and no message was to be found. She dressed, folded up the skirt and put it in a grocery sack. Outside, it was clear and hot, without a cloud. The breathless enormity of the Florida day entered her breathing self and made it light and pure. She could find him. The skirt was her excuse.

He wasn't at play practice, nor was anyone. A tolling bell reminded her: This was Sunday. She turned strange corners until she saw—far down a street in the ever-heating sunlight—a couple of shore patrols in white uniforms struggling with a man they were dragging out of a front walk between red flowers. The man's face was bruised with streaks of blood on it, the same as her own blood, red like the flowers. All down the street she could hear their heaving breath but no words . . . nothing to say.

She grew faint and around eleven-thirty went in a drugstore, sat down at the lunch counter and ate a sandwich. A fan was turning overhead. In a jar of pickling brine, some large eggs were floating. The man at the counter was darkly thinking of things not before him. The whiteness of the eggs in the huge jar frightened Dottie vaguely. From the mirror a smooth little face, her own, watched and noted that she looked about the same.

Move closer, or go far, she thought and folded her paper napkin. She knew which already. She paid her check and gathered up her bundle as responsibly as if it bore a child inside. She had wandered in: now, committed and compelled, she went a chosen way. She was lame, yes, and motherless, yes, and she'd been left with a legacy greater than she needed, but the one thing she knew she bore was a right to be seen, to be answered.

Everything, she guessed, was in the precise look of that big luxurious white stucco house when she finally found it by the blaze of the afternoon sun. She trudged in through the gate, her footsteps making unequal crushes into the gravel, her height not reaching halfway up the square sentinel posts of the entrance drive. The house looked blank, green-shuttered, sheltered and curtained and cool within. She remembered the patio, the pool, the trailing vines, thick as hair, a house with a woman inside whom she didn't like, an intricate mystery. In one sense she drove herself forward; in another, it was all she could possibly do. Her vital thread, whose touch was her life, was leading her.

From the upper floor windows, she supposed, you could see the water. The entrance was recessed into the shadow of an arch, and a grillwork gate of iron stood ajar before a closed front door of darkstained wood. A fan-like spread of steps led down to the gravel drive, and above them and below, a paving of square yellow tiles gave off a flat gloss to the sun. At either end of the tiled area below, large cement urns of verbena stood on square pedestals.

Clambering upward, step by halting step, she gained the entrance, but before approaching the door, she turned and looked around her. Out at the side where the pool was situated, she could see the coconut head of the Cuban, motionless, out of hearing. She walked three steps backward, and looked up to where on a balcony above stood the dark woman. She shielded her face from the sun.

"I thought you'd be at play practice," Dottie said.

"Not on Sunday. Wait there. I'm coming down."

Sandals on the long white walkways, the white-railed stairs, the marble floors, approaching expensively.

Then Dottie heard the sound of a car turning into the drive. She dropped the sack and ran.

Hidden behind a large stone urn full of verbena, Dottie watched as her enemy greeted Johnny at the door. Where did she go? Pam was probably asking him. Where did *who* go? You know, that girl you brought. The lame one. The *singer*, dopey.

Dottie looked up to where gazing down from an upper window the drunk blond grandmother was regarding her silently. When Pam and Johnny went inside, Dottie remained behind the verbena pot, alone and miserable, for even the old lady had closed the window, and the Cuban was out there asleep. He had to be asleep. Nobody could sit that still.

I want! I want! thought Dottie Almond; and alone, not just in that place but in the world, in the grand presence of her wishes, she turned and put her arms around the verbena urn and wet the harsh cement surface with streaming tears. Not only for Johnny but for herself, outside like that, and for her grand aplomb in seeing herself the possessor of the cool lovely house alone with him there in it, sometimes hidden from each other, wandering shadowy passages, sometimes discovering by chance or by search the other that each sought constantly, bedding for whole afternoons, and at night gathering moonlight in through windows, joining like twin divers in the pool, tangling like vines from sunny breakfasts onward, lords to the last fence corner and rock of gravel at the drive's head of all All *All.*

A drapery slid across a distant window, and Dottie limped out and away. Home. Nothing was merited; that, she knew. Nothing was ever deserved.

When, two days later, she saw him on the beach, he asked her where she'd been. "I thought about you," he said. "About the other night."

"What were you thinking?"

"How sweet you were." He touched her cheek, then caught her hand, and sat, holding it. "Why don't you come up to the university?" he said. "School's not far off. Morrissey can get you in."

"Pam's husband."

"Sure, Pam's husband. You met him. Morrissey."

"Pam—" she started, then gave out.

"What about Pam?" he asked.

"You're something—to her."

"I know I did a lot of talking the other night. Maybe I said things—things you didn't understand."

"Or maybe I did." Some force she didn't know the name of was pushing her on to the next thing to say. "Ron Morrissey—"

"What about him?"

"He got you out of something bad."

The boy did not answer.

"Is Johnny even your real name?"

He dropped his arm away and whereas before they

had been blending warm with each other while one breath did for both, he was now sitting separate from her, stoney silent. Dottie felt exhausted, like a sea creature who had struggled up on the beach, then to a rock, attaining, while the damp dried from its panting sides, a visible, singular identity. There wasn't any need to go farther.

"Come to practice," he said, and bent to kiss her.

"Be glad you're just crippled," they used to say, "you might be dead." "But why be either one?" she had asked.

From the beach she watched jet streams like scars fade into the sky. There was nothing left to do but pack her clothes, say goodbye to the room, get ready to take the bus all the way up Florida, across Alabama, all the way to North Mississippi in unbroken silence. And once on the road, she would drift in and out of sleep, thinking, Aunt Maggie Lee Asquith, it's you I'm riding with, Mr. Avery Donelson, I am travelling with you.

A FUGITIVE'S WIFE

The old lady now is getting me to read letters aloud to her; furthermore, I have to answer them. She is in charge of my soul at this point. Everything depends on her. Of course, she is going to take some advantages. That is to be expected.

. . . Dear Agnes paragraph indent if I do not write you more often please do not think that I am not always interested in you and your boys you are often in my thoughts do you know how to punctuate?

Yes, but now I have to start over (I am giggling at my own inattention) I wrote that in the letter.

To her it isn't funny. She isn't feeling at all well. She regards me as a bad child. I should be grateful, continually grateful. Instead, in a sense, I mock at her, whenever I behave carelessly, whenever I laugh.

Your new ballet shoes arrived. They're over there in the white box. From New Orleans.

Oh!

My true chord is struck. My self goes streaming toward the box, all on its toes. Restrained, I walk across to open the box, standing in repose in the classic third position I often take, heel in instep.

Pink!

Wasn't that what you ordered?

Perfect! I thought they'd send white instead.

Is your skirt pink?

I can dye it. I have before. You've got to get well for the program. . . .

Before we got the dance thing going at the Bozart, I was just a young mother with a beat-up Volkswagen and a little girl, driving to park in some bay up the beach alone, wandering afternoons among the clumps of seaweed, dodging the occasional person who wanted to talk, picking up driftwood. You can see it in advance, sanded, varnished, trimmed a little, angled to best advantage, ornamenting the chic coffee table at the cocktail hour. One day I made a good find, really remarkable, something that looked like two children with hands joined, tense and joyous with their playing. I must show it, was my impulse. Where? I sneaked it into the new development for the arts near the coast city whose name I was supposed never to mention. I've sneaked in here too, you realize, much like driftwood myself: mother, and daughter hardly walking yet, hardly talking yet (Where's *Dod-dee? When Dod-dee tummin?*)

It was there I saw the new dance stage. Chills went up and down me. I had studiously kept my leotards packed away, along with the satin slippers and the tulle skirt, the black practice shoes, the two costumes for productions at the Eastern college—"Graduation Ball" and Prokofieff's "Cinderella," my one starring part. My head began to whirl, silently orchestrating.

I stood before the window where the stage was, watching and waiting for someone to come who, I could see without speaking to them, would be in touch with what I knew. But no one came. The work on the stage was not going on and no class was then in session.

The boy in the design school, which had a shop opening onto the street, had been kind and responsive. Where are you from? Staying around here? Yes, it's good . . . I see what you see in it. Let me show you one we got last week. Maybe I'll put yours in the window.

Now I went back to him. Kathy is tired and fretting. I carry her. The ballet school. Oh, they're going to do all sorts of modern and folk dancing too, but they haven't got started. That's coming later. We had this huge grant, see? Instead of coming in a whoosh the money comes a little at a time, so we opened some shops to keep going, now it's fun, so we'll keep them. There's been a world of interest.

Cute advertising, I say.

Bozart? You like that?

Sure?

Y'all staying around here?

Yes and no. I smile in a don't-push-me way and he notices it. Not much difference between us, age-wise. We could for a moment be tableau stuff—mother, father, child. Except he's gay.

Next step, to rig up a practice bar, realize my happiness. Mrs. Levine, God help her, hasn't known how good she's had it. I'm going to worry that woman until I can dance again. She will fuss fuss fuss, but help me. She'll want it for me. She is kind and doomed. Those dark circles tell too much on her. Also the way she's come to say "Mary," in a personal tender way, a motherly or family way—that tells, too. It tells me I'll soon be tugging tights on, lacing shoes in place, lifting my arms in the old curving ways brought over here to us by those who cared about it.

Driftwood cannot be art . . . art is a discipline, not an accident. I am driftwood, but I can once again do what I was taught once . . . take my stance, lift my arms in curving grace, mount to my trembling toes.

At night, Kathy asleep, Mary sat with her leg tucked under her, writing to Bob.

Dear Johnny, Should I call you Johnny? All the girls do there, I'm sure, if it's the name you want. I've found a place to dance, an art center attached to a college. They've got some government money. I think I can work with the teacher if she's crazy enough to believe I'm hiding from a homicidal husband and don't want my name known. (Let's think of something better, can't we?) I'm counting days till you come. Kathy is fine. I've put up a practice bar out of an old length of iron pipe we got from a junk man. It isn't too bad now I've used rust remover and enameled it. I'm going to put up a little one for Kathy as soon as she can understand enough. She wants to imitate me already. How can you stand two geniuses? Mrs. L. has trepidations about the dancing, but I know she knows how lonely I've been, besotted in routine as bad as people who drink all the time or play bridge every day. There are some women up the beach who sit day in and day out on the front porch playing bridge. Pity I can't quit this and come crawl in bed with you. It will be next week and you won't let me down. Some day I want to meet your new friends there, too. It will do me good. They ought to think the world of this sacrifice I've made. Still, I've got to get word to Mom and Dad before too long. They've acted like they don't give a damn, but if anybody took Kathy away I would die. We'll talk about it. Mary.

She took the letter with her in the blue Volkswagen to mail to the secret box number at Marathon, above Key West. It seemed not a letter, but more like a little smoke signal sent up from behind her concealing hillside.

MR. McMILLAN

There are few sights more pleasant than a girl and a man dining happily together, and those two over in the corner were laughing as well that night, not too loudly but not softly either, because something was really funny, you had to suppose. In the courtyard restaurant out in the soft New Orleans September air, people spaced out among banana plants, lanterns, candlelight, palm trees, and a fish pool, turned from various distances and smiled.

Aline could soon be seen wiping her eyes on the big white napkin. It was an old habit, a tendency to cry when she laughed too much, and one which her whole family, she supposed, shared, for she could remember them all sitting through one perpetual summer after another in shorts and sandals on their screen porch, talking and telling things, and every once in a while bursting into such laughter that for a time no world would have been big enough to laugh in. So they would cry, great rolling salt tears as big as moth balls.

The man Aline was dining with apparently had no such family characteristic. He just quieted and refilled her wineglass.

"Good God," he said. "Incest, suicide, insanity, cancer, murder, divorce. Is that the best, really the best, you can do? I thought every Mississippi family had at least one idiot, two rapists, and a good criminal lawyer."

"I've only described my immediate family," she said. Whereupon they were both almost plunged back into merriment again, but the main course was set before them, a sizzling mass of flounder and shrimp.

"Of course," she said, lifting her fork, "I *love* them all."

"Well," he said soberly, "they sound very lovable."

She noticed he was doing very well with her, if that's what he wanted, and evidently he did. From now on they would have a note, a tone, to return to; they could share a knowledge that life was funny and serious both at once, the way, to her, it really was. He had wired her up home, up in Mississippi, from Chicago. In the old days, the wire would have been called up or run up from the station and everybody in town would have known what was in it before it reached her. But now that the new exchanges had been put in, the message had been telephoned out to her impersonally from a point some thirty miles away. She had told her family it had been about her research at the university, that one of the department assistants was sick and a report was due right after Labor Day. She didn't want to talk about him, the young man she'd met three months ago at a convention in Indiana. If she laid it to her work, which was taking her eight years to train for, having to do with disease-carrying parasites in South American

countries, they merely nodded. They never asked her anything about it, even when she had seen the light of what
she could really do in the world and what she loved, and
had determined to make for it, like a swimmer choosing a
distant goal. Full of enthusiasm, with a fellowship promised her after graduation, she had come home and tried to
explain. One by one she saw those faces, so like her own,
turn glum, and dollar signs, as if in comic strips, appeared
to grow on their eyeballs. As stuffed with money as piggy
banks, they appeared for the first time to show how they'd
earned it, by letting it be a prime motive in everything.
Why hadn't she married as any pretty girl should? She
would be further from it, now, with every year that passed.
And she wouldn't even be earning. It did not matter how
her face was glowing. She might as well have announced
to them that she was going into anything, from Aristote-
lian philosophy to codifying puberty rites among African
tribes. It was all the same to them. "We just don't know
anything about it," was what they had said when she (a girl:
imagine!) had determined on a science major. It was what
they said now when she wanted to go further—a good
answer, she supposed, for next to everything. On the second day they had started complaining; she could expect
nothing, they had decided, beyond that fellowship, since it
was so grand and pleased her so. On the third, they having
got together again, she was the butt of ridicule, needled at
table, ignored in hallways. She'd no old uncle or cousin or
aunt out in the country to go and talk to, for heart's ease

and understanding: they had died. But the uncle had left her a small wooded acreage near town. She had wanted to turn it into a town park someday, but needing money, she went secretly and mortgaged it, and, check in hand, heartsick, young, dashed, determining on the train not to think about it, to get that stricken look off her face, she had returned to New Orleans. No need to go home at all, she thought, unless they needed her.

But she did go back, from time to time. She would get to feeling bad about them and then, as two years had gone and thanks to no one up there she was actually making it, with her glow about it all intact as well, she would get to feeling something else. Her very capacity to pull through must have come, in some way, from them. If not, how could she love them still? They had wrecked her little piece of land: it was an accident. The lumber company they had contracted to cut timber off their own property had assumed hers part of theirs. When they'd noticed, they said, it was too late. Timber lost, the man who'd lent against her mortgage wanted out, and worst of all, the beautiful glade was spoiled for the next fifty years. Who had cared enough to keep things straight? When she thought of it, she would knot her fists, nails digging at her palms, wondering: What went with our laughter? Why don't we laugh any more? And big family-size tears would roll off into her pillow.

She believed in self-knowledge, even though trying to find it in the bosom of a Mississippi family was like trying to find some object lost in a gigantic attic, when you really didn't know what you were looking for. Why look at all? she wondered. Most of her traits she'd learned away from them. One was how not to talk all the time. She now retired into silence. It was he who got to talking then, and kept it up, interesting enough, witty enough, certainly happy to be with her, straight on through coffee and dessert and cigarette and out to his car and into the French Quarter where everybody on earth was walking around, even a group of Scots in kilts playing bagpipes. They got pushed apart time and again on the narrow streets.

"I think people must be wilder down here," he observed. "Of course, in Chicago when you feel wild you go out and shoot to kill. But for the reasons you have to read the papers, then you don't know."

"I'm sure that nobody you know shoots anybody," she kindly said.

"Hate to disappoint you. Some of my best friends—"

A couple of bars, a couple of drinks later, the evening began to drift around them like the river, broad and lazy; they drove around the park and then out to the lake, watching swans and colored fountains.

"Why are you living in that ruin?" he asked her, walking along the lake and angling kisses at her, now and then.

"I'm not. I came back a day early to see you and just went there. I didn't want Ann and Helen to know you were here, I guess. Those are the girls I—"

"Oh, I remember. They come out in hair curlers, dragging on cigarettes. You'd think you were still in college."

"They do make me feel that way. I stay there because it's cheap. I really can't afford anything different." She hesitated. "Do you have to save?"

"No, I guess I've always been lucky." A breeze blew. He wound his arm around her waist. She walked along a parapet, holding to his shoulder. "Money's never worried me," he confessed.

"When I came back here after the family wouldn't see why I wanted this career, I stayed a few days at what you call that old ruin. It really isn't a ruin, just an old pile of a Victorian residence. Somebody turned it into a hotel. Well, you saw the entrance hall, that great big stairway, so you know what it's like all over."

"That Moorish pin-up on the landing, stripped to the waist and holding a lamp—God, how can you stand it?"

"I just went there at first because it was near Tulane."

"Then you got sentimental about it. Couldn't wait to get back."

"No, it wasn't that." They were in the car again and she straightened up, drawing herself free of his arms, sitting away from him, arranging her hair. The gentle haze of alcohol was fading. She said: "I just go there because of Mr. McMillan."

"Mr. McMillan? So there is somebody you like."

"Nothing like that—not a boy friend."

"What then?" He was smiling, both within and without, asking himself, Am I sliding into a lifetime of listening to stories? He must not have felt it such a hardship, this being the third time he'd found himself all the way down here for no other reason than Aline. He'd marked her first as a pretty, still face in a knot of rattling Southerners at the Indianapolis convention, one face in a crowded hotel lobby. What was there about it? A strain pushing up beneath a calm surface—anxiety? desire?—hinted at what might be interesting about her, what tugged his attention to her.

"Mr. McMillan came from up in Mississippi, too, like me. I never saw him. He had had a whole life in some little town, married this girl everybody expected him to marry as her life would have been ruined, she'd have been nothing but an old maid, if he hadn't, sent two children through school, cared for both parents till they died, cared for her—loved her, too, I guess—till she died, and then quietly having given all his life up to sixty-odd to doing just what everybody thought he ought to do and being all the time sincere—loving instead of hating, you know—he just calmly came down here and took a room for a night or so at that old hotel and never left."

"Then he must be there still. Or did he die?"

"Yes, he died, just about the time I came myself, though nobody would have mentioned that to a new guest. They had found him one morning after he died in his sleep, and they set about getting a doctor, telephoning up to that town to find out his children's names and notifying them, finding an undertaker—oh, they did everything without stint. And then the son and the son's wife came down on the train and went back with the coffin, northward, but nobody followed—just didn't go, somehow. If the ones left who had known him all along spoke of him, I don't know what they said. I came in and didn't know anything had happened, though the first day, once I looked back on it, there had been some sort of commotion, people talking in the TV lounge and others being called aside when they came in from work, into the little office where the switchboard is—it must have been a butler's pantry back in the old days—and at night a going up and down steps and a knock at certain doors. But I remembered all this later like something that happened while I dreamed. I wouldn't have noticed that one of the guests had gone for a day or so.

"I knew when he reappeared only by coincidence, because in the middle of a hot, still September afternoon I had come into that cool old hallway, spacious and dim as a church but freed of everything like duty and being holy. I had got to the desk and was looking around for somebody to ask for the key and for whatever mail or calls there'd been, when the lady who sometimes keeps the desk came out of the switchboard room and looked straight past me, her look went like a bullet, and I saw something like shock or strain on her face, but not either one—you'd have to call it recognition. I turned and there stood an elderly gentleman with nearly white hair whom I'd got glimpses of when I first arrived. He had the air of a traveler returned from a mission and he carried something the size of a box of candy under his arm. He held it out to her. 'It's him,' he said. She looked at it and nodded. It was such a singular thing, so intense. They really didn't know I was there, were so taken up they couldn't be conscious of anything beyond their own knowing. 'It's Mr. McMillan,' he said."

"In the box?"

Aline nodded.

"Cremated?"

She nodded again.

"Ashes to ashes," he remarked, looking out over Lake Pontchartrain, the night having swung close to its deeper hours, noting the distant lights of fishing boats, lonely, solitary with the knowledge of work continued in the forgetfulness of everybody else.

"He didn't return to dust or ashes either, not in the long run. Listen. He had let them bury him up there, let them do the whole thing. Then they read the will and found the envelope attached to the will and the letter inside saying what he really wanted. So then they called down to New Orleans, to the hotel. Mr. McMillan had been in the war. Scarcely under the age limit, at the time— thirty-eight or thirty-nine—he could have got out of it without even trying to, but he insisted he wanted to go. He went to Hawaii—Pearl Harbor—on something called Eastern reconnaissance, which meant, in his case anyway, that he traveled from the Pearl Harbor army base across to ships and took messages from the Army to the Navy and vice versa about what each knew that the other didn't. He covered the bay over and over, never knowing what information he carried or what effect it had on anybody, what lives were saved or lost because of it, or what file it finally wound up in. But he got to know the bay and he got to know the islands, and he loved it all apparently, though he never talked much about it. Being older than most veterans, he never hung around with buddies when he came home, or joined any of the groups, but when he died, he had quietly decided, he wanted his ashes scattered on that water. It was only a case of finding somebody who would do it for him, as nobody in that little town or in the family would have known what to make of such a request and would have probably decided right away that he was crazy for even asking it, but he asked them to notify the hotel and said that somebody there would take the envelope containing his request and the money for the trip. He didn't specify who it would be, not even man or woman. He just knew somebody would. And they did. Would you say it was just for a free ticket to Hawaii?"

"No, I wouldn't say that. Neither would you. He'd found his own sort, the people he wanted to do things for him, and then they did it. I guess all of life is worth that."

The dark had really come down on them. She could barely see his face.

"Up there where the family was, they didn't seem to care any more, once the funeral was over. It just became something after the fact, everything being settled for them when they had transferred the property and paid the undertaker. I guess after everything, every single thing, and every person is served, then you can have what you really want."

"You sound bitter," he said. "Why look at the world like that?"

"From failing, like he did. In a way I envied him. They got through doing all the things about his death that they expected of themselves. Then they saw the will and the letter inside, and the stranger. So they let him be dug up and carted off and burned to ashes and carried away like that— in a little box. And they didn't care. They didn't care at all." She was laughing.

"Don't laugh like that. It's late; you're tired."

Well, that was true, she thought, letting herself be drawn closely in, giving in to the all but strange face whose exact features up to the very reappearance of him that afternoon she could not recall. Mysteriously, his outline took firm life against her; even stranger, it seemed entirely right that it should do so—should be as it was, and more, should be all it intended to be. What is flesh and blood, she wondered, but what it seems right to be close to?

But when she shut her eyes at last, she heard in her head the silken wash and fall of Hawaiian water, and the night breeze that lay against her cheek was of that climate.

GO SOUTH IN THE WINTER

Mrs. Landis came out into the morning sun of the West Indies in bathing suit and robe, seeking her beach chair before the Caribe Hilton in San Juan. She arranged her possessions around her, book and beach bag containing her cap, cosmetics, and wallet, then draped her towel on the back of the chair, and having smeared herself with sun-protective lotion, opened her book and began to read. She soon became sleepy (at the same time as her husband a thousand miles to the north was sleepy also: he suffered from a mild hangover and was disinclined to tackle his income tax). Sun drowsiness was Mrs. Landis' reason, and she welcomed it; she liked to doze in sunlight.

A wrangle of voices stirred her from her mood and she looked up. The young Jewish couple she had conversed with the day before were back, complete with baby in sun bonnet. Each time they turned the baby loose it came to her. Sandy, it clambered over her knees, pushed her book out of her hands, examined her face at close range, and seizing her hair by the fistful, shook her with real force.

"Sonia!"

Both parents called to her, and the young mother rose to fetch her, detaching her from Mrs. Landis a finger at a time. "She doesn't hurt, let her play," Mrs. Landis protested, laughing.

"She's got Mrs. Landis mixed up with her grandmother, I think. Don't you think so, George?" The young mother swung the baby free. "It's absolutely clear."

"Must be: they look alike," her husband agreed. He piled sand for the baby, who wanted strenuously to go back to Mrs. Landis and now began to cry.

"Did you see the show last night, Mrs. Landis?" the girl asked. She was dark, interested, relaxed, plump, her hair screwed up behind to keep her neck bare for sunning and swimming, a large floppy native straw hat set forward on her brow.

"The dancing? Just the beginning. I went up early."

"They were good, you know."

"Yeah, you shoulda stayed," the young man said.

The baby continued to wail and struggle to return to Mrs. Landis. The father held it, like an animal in harness, by the cross straps of its cotton sun suit.

"I'm here alone," said Mrs. Landis, "so that makes it—"

Here the baby's crying grew strident with demand, and the young couple turned to consult each other. "You'd better take her in," the wife agreed. The young man got up and carried the child toward the water. Halfway there she noticed the sea and leaned toward it, jumping to get to it faster.

What was I going to say? Mrs. Landis wondered. "That makes it . . ." What? She didn't know. Makes it difficult to be alone at floor shows? In former years she had tried conversations with various strangers—couples, other loners—and sometimes these had worked out pleasantly. Why didn't she want to do that now? On the other hand, why should she?

The reasons for doing anything were lacking for her, she reflected, at this particular period of her life. But after all, she'd come there just to drift, to do nothing she didn't feel inclined to do. She idly recalled the middle-aged divorcé she had some years back allowed to talk his way into her bed. She watched the gulls drift, turn, flap wings, soar, and drift again. On an arm of the beach, far out, the palms blew. The young father was floating his baby in the sea. It flailed arms and legs, making wild splashes, yelping with glee. What a violent child! Mrs. Landis thought, and at the same instant was startled as it leaped so high that, momentarily free of the water, it seemed magnified by a trick of vision into something larger than life, the painting of a baby, huge on a master canvas which contained, as minor objects, trees, sea, and clouds.

Mrs. Landis wondered if she would be feeling less detached if she were at home. She liked to play bridge but if deprived of the pleasure she would not have missed it much. Volunteer duty at the hospital did not utterly absorb her. She knew that her husband, though retirement had left him with little to say, still needed her. Her children telephoned and visited; her grandchildren wrote; her friends were faithful; and people who got to know her usually liked and admired her.

Arranging her hair where the baby had pulled it down, she rubbed lotion on her back and along the underside of her arms and legs. Then flattening the chair and balancing her body so as not to tip over, she turned to lie on her face.

Behind her, the young family were talking, the father having returned with the dripping child fresh from the sea; they were spreading down large beach towels for her to play on. Now they were switching on a transistor radio; Mrs. Landis heard the spiel of selected news items from the States and abroad which would be repeated in more or less the same form all day until around five o'clock, when new releases would be substituted. There went the latest Presidential primary, next came the Middle East, now a new White House appointment, then the latest in scandal and corruption. Mrs. Landis half-dozed.

She thought of her children, thought of her oldest boy when he was four or five and how she had found she could talk to him, converse with him, as one might to an adult, and how this discovery had been a great delight. In her memory they were walking, the two of them, along a road in Vermont. The fresh June green of maple and beech trees shadowed them; roadside bushes mingled with wild white and yellow flowers. The boy walked ahead of her, talking eagerly. His thoughts came out the instant he had them, no self-consciousness to stop or deflect them: what a joy this was! Near the top of a hill, rain overtook them from behind, a tough sudden downpour with a sharp wind. An empty house stood just off the road, so they climbed a fence and ran for it. Here they sheltered, under a porch roof half-fallen in. Lilacs overgrown and unpruned bloomed among the ruins. First lashed about and drenched, the branches then stood still and poured out fragrance; soon the sun came out again. Her son had talked constantly until half-way through the storm when he had finished all he had to say, then closed his mouth in that sudden serious way he was all his life to retain, though that one day it seemed to crystallize forever in her heart's thought of him. Was it the baby clambering about on her which had brought back all this treasure, at once warm yet inaccessible?

She had almost fallen asleep. Behind her, the news went on—most of it now from New York. An art gallery theft, a prediction of snow, the mayor's latest national pronouncement, a city commissioner's death, killed in a traffic accident coming from Kennedy Airport. His name was Landis. Landis. They said it three times, each with a blur of words between. Landis.

Mrs. Landis, who had never before heard of the man who had died, sat straight up. Tears streamed out from underneath her dark glasses, poured down through the lotion on her face. Her hand moved helplessly to conceal or stop them. The young couple had sat up to look at her. They were people who missed nothing. She had seen them only once, the day before, yet her name had been produced the minute they saw her. Now they had caught the thread at once, and were looking at her with alarm.

"Not what you think," she wanted to reassure them, but all she managed actually to say was: "My son . . . oh no!"

"Oh no!" the young wife echoed. "To hear it on the radio!"

The young man said nothing. He came forward at once, straightening from his knees up. Though apparently about to rise, he seemed, like a figure in a ritual, to be kneeling to her, arms outstretched.

"No, don't," said Mrs. Landis. She groped, gathering up book, beach bag, and towel and walked unsteadily away, leaving them behind. Halfway to the hotel, the young man caught up with her.

"Do you want anybody? Need anything? Can I—?"

"No . . . please, I—" She stumbled on and he stopped and turned back.

It had all happened in the sun, she thought. The strong, almighty sun—everywhere at once, beneficent, fierce, impersonal—what they'd come to find. She had not thought of it as a presence until she left it, felt it slip from her as she entered the hotel terraces. In her room she finished crying, bathed her face and showered, and stood at last in a fresh linen dress, overlooking the whole scene from her balcony: the beach, the palms waving, and the young couples taking their children down by either hand to go into the sea.

Late in the afternoon she sought out the two who had seen her cry. She sat down and talked to them in a charming, open way, confessing everything.

"I happened to be dreaming about my son when he was a boy, then this news came in the middle of it about a man completely unrelated. Dreaming, but not dreaming . . . can you understand?"

"It tripped the switch," the young man said.

"We've been worried about you all day, Mrs. Landis," his wife said gravely.

"Thank you for being so kind," Mrs. Landis said. She was laughing, a woman sometimes foolish, but now restored to the smooth, safe surfaces. She said that she would come that night, to watch the dancing.

SHIP ISLAND

The Story of a Mermaid

The French book was lying open on a corner of the dining room table, between the floor lamp and the window. The floor lamp, which had come with the house, had a cover made of green glass, with a fringe. The French book must have lain just that way for two months. Nancy, coming in from the beach, tried not to look at it. It reminded her of how much she had meant to accomplish during the summer, of the strong sense of intent, something like refinement, with which she had chosen just that spot for studying. It was out of hearing of the conversations with the neighbors that went on every evening out on the side porch, it had window light in the daytime and lamplight at night, it had a small, slanting view of the beach, and it drew a breeze. The pencils were still there, still sharp, and the exercise, broken off. She sometimes stopped to read it over. "The soldiers of the emperor were crossing the bridge: *Les soldats de l'empereur traversaient le pont.* The officer has already knocked at the gate: *L'officier a déjà frappé—"* She could not have finished that sentence now if she had sat right down and tried.

Nancy could no longer find herself in relation to the girl who had sought out such a good place to study, had sharpened the pencils and opened the book and sat down to bend over it. What she did know was how—just now, when she had been down at the beach, across the boulevard—the sand scuffed beneath her step and shells lay strewn about, chipped and disorderly, near the water's edge. Some shells were empty; some, with damp drying down their backs, went for short walks. Far out, a long white shelf of cloud indicated a distance no gull could dream of gaining, though the gulls spun tirelessly up, dazzling in the white light that comes just as morning vanishes. A troop of pelicans sat like curiously carved knobs on the tops of a long series of wooden piles, which were spaced out at intervals in the water. The piles were what was left of a private pier blown away by a hurricane some years ago.

Nancy had been alone on the beach. Behind her, the boulevard glittered in the morning sun and the season's traffic rocked by the long curve of the shore in clumps that seemed to burst, then speed on. She stood looking outward at the high straight distant shelf of cloud. The islands were out there, plainly visible. The walls of the old Civil War fort on the nearest one of them, the one with the lighthouse—Ship Island—were plain today as well. She had been out there once this summer with Rob Acklen, out there on the island, where the reeds grew in the wild white sand, and the water teemed so thick with seaweed that only crazy people would have tried to swim in it. The gulf had rushed white and strong through all the seaweed, frothing up the beach. On the beach, the froth turned brown, the color of softly moving crawfish claws. In the boat coming home through the sunset that day, a boy standing up in the pilot-house played "Over the Waves" on his harmonica. Rob Acklen had put his jacket around Nancy's shoulders—she had never thought to bring a sweater. The jacket swallowed her; it smelled more like Rob than he did. The boat moved, the breeze blew, the sea swelled, all to the lilt of the music. The twenty-five members of the Laurel, Mississippi, First Baptist Church Adult Bible Class, who had come out with them on the excursion boat, and to whom Rob and Nancy had yet to introduce themselves, had stopped giggling and making their silly jokes. They were tired, and stood in a huddle like sheep; they were shaped like sheep as well, with little shoulders and wide bottoms—it was somehow sad. Nancy and Rob, young and trim, stood side by side near the bow, like figureheads of the boat, hearing the music and watching the thick prow butt the swell, which the sunset had stained a deep red. Nancy felt for certain that this was the happiest she had ever been.

Alone on the sand this morning, she had spread out her beach towel and stood for a moment looking up the beach, way up, past a grove of live oaks to where Rob Acklen's house was visible. He would be standing in the kitchen, in loafers and a dirty white shirt and an old pair of shorts, drinking cold beer from the refrigerator right out of the can. He would eat lunch with his mother and sister, read the paper and write a letter, then dress and drive into town to help his father in the office, going right past Nancy's house along the boulevard. Around three, he would call her up. He did this every day. His name was Fitzrobert Conroy Acklen—one of those full-blown Confederate names. Everybody liked him, and more than a few—a general mixture of every color, size, age, sex, and religion—would say when he passed by, "I declare, I just love that boy." So he was bound to have a lot of nicknames: "Fitz" or "Bobbie" or "Cousin" or "Son"—he answered to almost anything. He was the kind of boy people have high, undefined hopes for. He had first seen Nancy Lewis one morning when he came by her house to make an insurance call for his father.

Breaking off her French—could it have been the sentence about "*l'officier*"?—she had gone out to see who it was. She was expecting Mrs. Nattier, their neighbor, who had skinny white freckled legs she never shaved and whose husband, "off" somewhere, was thought not to be doing well; or Mrs. Nattier's little boy Bernard, who thought it was fun to hide around corners after dark and jump out saying nothing more original than "Boo!" (once, he had screamed "Raw head and bloody bones!" but Nancy was sure somebody had told him to); or one of the neighbor ladies in the back—old Mrs. Poultney, whom they rented from and who walked with a cane, or Miss Henriette Dupré, who was so devout she didn't even have to go to confession before weekday Communion and whose hands, always tucked up in the sleeves of her sack, were as cold as church candles, and to think of them touching you was like rabbits skipping over your grave on dark rainy nights in winter up in the lonely wet-leaf-covered hills. Or else it was somebody wanting to be paid something. Nancy had opened the door and looked up, and there, instead of a dozen other people, was Rob Acklen.

Not that she knew his name. She had seen boys like him down on the coast, ever since her family had moved there from Little Rock back in the spring. She had seen them playing tennis on the courts back of the hotel, where she sometimes went to jump on the trampoline. She believed that the hotel people thought she was on the staff in some sort of way, as she was about the right age for that—just a year or so beyond high school but hardly old enough to work in town. The weather was already getting hot, and the season was falling off. When she passed the courts, going and coming, she saw the boys out of the corner of her eye. Were they really so much taller than the boys up where they had moved from, up in Arkansas? They were lankier and a lot more casual. They were more assured. To Nancy, whose family was in debt and whose father, in one job after another, was always doing something wrong, the boys playing tennis had that wonderful remoteness of creatures to be admired on the screen, or those seen in whiskey ads, standing near the bar of a country club and sleekly talking about things she could not begin to imagine. But now here was one, in a heavy tan cotton suit and a light blue shirt with a buttoned-down collar and dark tie, standing on her own front porch and smiling at her.

Yet when Rob called Nancy for a date, a day or two later, she didn't have to be told that he did it partly because he liked to do nice things for people. He obviously liked to be considerate and kind, because the first time he saw her he said, "I guess you don't know many people yet?"

"No, because Daddy just got transferred," she said— "transferred" being her mother's word for it; fired was what it was. She gave him a Coke and talked to him awhile, standing around in the house, which unaccountably continued to be empty. She said she didn't know a thing about insurance.

Now, still on the beach, Nancy Lewis sat down in the middle of her beach towel and began to rub suntan lotion on her neck and shoulders. Looking down the other way, away from Rob's house and toward the yacht club, she saw a man standing alone on the sand. She had not noticed him before. He was facing out toward the gulf and staring fixedly at the horizon. He was wearing shorts and a shirt made out of red bandanna, with the tail out—a stout young man with black hair.

Just then, without warning, it began to rain. There were no clouds one could see in the overhead dazzle, but it rained anyway; the drops fell in huge discs, marking the sand, and splashing on Nancy's skin. Each drop seemed enough to fill a Dixie cup. At first, Nancy did not know what the stinging sensation was; then she knew the rain was burning her. It was scalding hot! Strange, outlandish, but also painful, was how she found it. She jumped up and began to flinch and twist away, trying to escape, and a moment later she had snatched up her beach towel and flung it around her shoulders. But the large hot drops kept falling, and there was no escape from them. She started rubbing her cheek and forehead and felt that she might blister all over; then, since it kept on and on and was all so inexplicable, she grabbed her lotion and ran up the beach and out of the sand and back across the boulevard. Once in her own front yard, under the scraggy trees, she felt the rain no longer, and looked back curiously into the dazzle beyond the boulevard.

"I thought you meant to stay for a while," her mother said. "Was it too hot? Anybody would be crazy to go out there now. There's never anybody out there at this time of day."

"It was all right," said Nancy, "but it started raining. I never felt anything like it. The rain was so hot it burned me. Look. My face—" She ran to look in the mirror. Sure enough, her face and shoulders looked splotched. It might blister. I might be scarred for life, she thought—one of those dramatic phrases left over from high school.

Nancy's mother, Mrs. Lewis, was a discouraged lady whose silky, blondish-gray hair was always slipping loose and tagging out around her face. She would not try to improve herself and talked a lot in company about her family; two of her uncles had been professors simultaneously at the University of North Carolina. One of them had written a book on phonetics. Mrs. Lewis seldom found anyone who had heard of them, or of the book, either. Some people asked what phonetics were, and others did not ask anything at all.

Mrs. Lewis now said to her daughter, "You just got too much sun."

"No, it was the rain. It was really scalding hot."

"I never heard of such a thing," her mother said. "Out of a clear sky."

"I can't help that," Nancy said. "I guess I ought to know."

Mrs. Lewis took on the kind of look she had when she would open the handkerchief drawer of a dresser and see two used, slightly bent carpet nails, some Scotch Tape melted together, an old receipt, an unanswered letter announcing a cousin's wedding, some scratched negatives saved for someone but never developed, some dusty foreign coins, a bank deposit book from a town they lived in during the summer before Nancy was born, and an old telegram whose contents, forgotten, no one would dare now to explore, for it would say something awful but absolutely true.

"I wish you wouldn't speak to me like that," Mrs. Lewis said. "All I know is, it certainly didn't rain here."

Nancy wandered away, into the dining room. She felt bad about everything—about quarreling with her mother, about not getting a suntan, about wasting her time all summer with Rob Acklen and not learning any French. She went and took a long cool bath in the big old bathroom, where the bathtub had ball-and-claw feet painted mustard yellow and the single light bulb on the long cord dropped down one mile from the stratosphere.

What the Lewises found in a rented house was always outclassed by what they brought into it. Nancy's father, for instance, had a china donkey that bared its teeth in a great big grin. Written on one side was "If you really want to look like me" and on the other "Just keep right on talking." Her father loved the donkey and its message, and always put it on the living room table of whatever house they were in. When he got a drink before dinner each evening he would wander back with glass in hand and look the donkey over. "That's pretty good," he would say just before he took the first swallow. Nancy had often longed to break the donkey, by accident—that's what she would say, that it had all been an accident—but she couldn't get over the feeling that if she did, worse things than the Lewises had ever imagined would happen to them. That donkey would let in a flood of trouble, that she knew.

After Nancy got out of the tub and dried, she rubbed Jergens Lotion on all the splotches the rain had made. Then she ate a peanut-butter sandwich and more shrimp salad left over from supper the night before, and drank a cold Coke. Now and then, eating, she would go look in the mirror. By the time Rob Acklen called up, the red marks had all but disappeared.

That night, riding down to Biloxi with Rob, Nancy confided that the catalogue of people she disliked, headed by Bernard Nattier, included every single person—Miss Henriette Dupré, Mrs. Poultney, and Mrs. Nattier, and Mr. Nattier, too, when he was at home—that she had to be with these days. It even included, she was sad to say, her mother and father. If Bernard Nattier had to be mean—and it was clear he did have to—why did he have to be so corny? He put wads of wet, chewed bubble gum in her purses—that was the most original thing he ever did. Otherwise, it was just live crawfish in her bed or crabs in her shoes; anybody could think of that. And when he stole, he took things *she* wanted, nothing simple, like money—she could have forgiven him for that—but cigarettes, lipstick, and ashtrays she had stolen herself here and there. If she locked her door, he got in through the window; if she locked the window, she suffocated. Not only that, but he would crawl out from under the bed. His eyes were slightly crossed and he knew how to turn the lids back on themselves so that it looked like blood, and then he would chase her. He was browned to the color of dirt all over and he smelled like salt mud the sun had dried. He wore black tennis shoes laced too tight at the ankles and from sunup till way past dark he never thought of anything but what to do to Nancy, and she would have liked to kill him.

She made Rob Acklen laugh. She amused him. He didn't take anything Nancy Lewis could say at all to heart, but, as if she was something he had found on the beach and was teaching to talk, he, with his Phi Beta Kappa key and his good level head and his wonderful prospects, found everything she told about herself cute, funny, absurd. He did remark that he had such feelings himself from time to time—that he would occasionally get crazy mad at one of his parents or the other, and that he once planned his sister's murder down to the last razor slash. But he laughed again, and his chewing gum popped amiably in his jaws. When she told him about the hot rain, he said he didn't believe it. He said, "Aw," which was what a boy like Rob Acklen said when he didn't believe something. The top of his old white Mercury convertible was down and the wind rushed past like an endless bolt of raw silk being drawn against Nancy's cheek.

In the ladies' room mirror at the Beach View, where they stopped to eat, she saw the bright quality of her eyes, as though she had been drinking. Her skirts rustled in the narrow room; a porous white disc of deodorant hung on a hook, fuming the air. Her eyes, though blue, looked startlingly dark in her pale skin, for though she tried hard all the time, she never seemed to tan. All the sun did, as her mother was always pointing out, was bleach her hair three shades lighter; a little more and it would be almost white.

Out on the island that day, out on Ship Island, she had drifted in the water like seaweed, with the tide combing her limbs and hair, tugging her through lengths of fuzzy water growth. She had lain flat on her face with her arms stretched before her, experiencing the curious lift the water's motion gave to the tentacles of weed, wondering whether she liked it or not. Did something alive clamber over the small of her back? Did something wishful grope the spiral of her ear? Rob had caught her wrist hard and waked her—waked was what he did, though to sleep in the water is not possible. He said he thought she had been there too long. "Nobody can keep their face in the water that long," was what he said.

"I did," said Nancy.

Rob's brow had been blistered a little, she recalled, for that had been back early in the summer, soon after they had met—but the changes the sun made on him went without particular attention. The seasons here were old ground to him. He said that the island was new, however—or at least forgotten. He said he had never been there but once, and that many years ago, on a Boy Scout picnic. Soon they were exploring the fort, reading the dates off the metal signs whose letters glowed so smoothly in the sun, and the brief summaries of what those little boys, little military-academy boys turned into soldiers, had endured. Not old enough to fill up the name of soldier, or of prisoner, either, which is what they were— not old enough to shave, Nancy bet—still, they had died there, miserably far from home, and had been buried in the sand. There was a lot more. Rob would have been glad to read all about it, but she wasn't interested. What they knew already was plenty, just about those boys. A bright, worried lizard ran out of a hot rubble of brick. They came out of the fort and walked alone together eastward toward the dunes, now skirting near the shore that faced the sound and now wandering south, where they could hear or sometimes glimpse the gulf. They were overlooked all the way by an old white lighthouse. From far away behind, the twenty-five members of the adult Bible class could be overheard playing a silly, shrill Sunday-school game. It came across the ruins of the fort and the sad story of the dead soldiers like something that had happened long ago that you could not quite remember having joined in. On the beach to their right, toward the gulf, a flock of sandpipers with blinding-white breasts stepped pecking along the water's edge, and on the inner beach, toward the sound, a wrecked sailboat with a broken mast lay half buried in the sand.

Rob kept teasing her along, pulling at the soft wool strings of her bathing suit, which knotted at the nape and again under her shoulder blades, worrying loose the damp hair that she had carefully slicked back and pinned. "There isn't anybody in that house," he assured her, some minutes later, having explored most of that part of the island and almost as much of Nancy as well, having almost, but not quite—his arms around her—coaxed and caressed her down to ground level in a clump of reeds. "There hasn't been in years and years," he said, encouraging her.

"It's only those picnic people," she said, holding off, for the reeds would not have concealed a medium-sized mouse. They had been to look at the sailboat and thought about climbing inside (kissing closely, they had almost fallen right over into it), but it did have a rotten tin can in the bottom and smelled, so here they were back out in the dunes.

"They've got to drink all those Coca-Colas," Rob said, "and give out all those prizes, and anyway—"

She never learned anyway what, but it didn't matter. Maybe she began to make up for all that the poor little soldiers had missed out on, in the way of making love. The island's very spine, a warm reach of thin ground, came smoothly up into the arch of her back; and it was at least halfway the day itself, with its fair, wide-open eyes, that she went over to. She felt somewhat historical afterward, as though they had themselves added one more mark to all those that place remembered.

Having played all the games and given out the prizes, having eaten all the homemade cookies and drunk the case of soft drinks just getting warm, and gone sight-seeing through the fort, the Bible class was now coming, too, crying "Yoohoo!" to explore the island. They discovered Rob hurling shells and bits of rock into the surf, while Nancy, scavenging a little distance away, tugged up out of the sand a shell so extraordinary it was worth showing around. It was purple, pink, and violet inside—a palace of colors; the king of the oysters had no doubt lived there. When she held it shyly out to them, they cried "Look!" and "Ooo!" so there was no need for talking to them much at all, and in the meantime the evening softened, the water glowed, the glare dissolved. Far out, there were other islands one could see now, and beyond those must be many more. They had been there all along.

Going home, Nancy gave the wonderful shell to the boy who stood in the pilothouse playing "Over the Waves." She glanced back as they walked off up the pier and saw him look at the shell, try it for weight, and then throw it in the water, leaning far back on his arm and putting a good spin on the throw, the way boys like to do—the way Rob Acklen himself had been doing, too, just that afternoon.

"Why did you do that?" Rob had demanded. He was frowning; he looked angry. He had thought they should keep the shell—to remember, she supposed.

"For the music," she explained.

"But it was ours," he said. When she didn't answer, he said again, "Why did you, Nancy?"

But still she didn't answer.

When Nancy returned to their table at the Beach View, having put her lipstick back straight after eating fish, Rob was paying the check. "Why not believe me?" she asked him. "It was true. The rain was hot as fire. I thought I would be scarred for life."

It was still broad daylight, not even twilight. In the bright, air-conditioned restaurant, the light from the water glazed flatly against the broad picture windows, the chandeliers, and the glasses. It was the hour when mirrors reflect nothing and bars look tired. The restaurant was a boozy, cheap sort of place with a black-lined gambling hall in the back, but everyone went there because the food was good.

"You're just like Mama," she said. "You think I made it up."

Rob said, teasing, "I didn't say that. I just said I didn't believe it." He loved getting her caught in some sort of logic she couldn't get out of. When he opened the door for her, she got a good sidelong view of his longish, firm face and saw the way his somewhat fine brows arched up with one or two bright reddish hairs in among the dark ones; his hair was that way, too, when the sun hit it. Maybe, if nobody had told him, he wouldn't have known it; he seemed not to notice so very much about himself. Having the confidence of people who don't worry much, his grin could snare her instantly—a glance alone could make her feel how lucky she was he'd ever noticed her. But it didn't do at all to think about him now. It would be ages before they made it through the evening and back, retracing the way and then turning off to the bayou, and even then, there would be those mosquitoes.

Bayou love-making suited Rob just fine; he was one of those people mosquitoes didn't bite. They certainly bit

Nancy. They were huge and silent, and the minute the car stopped they would even come and sit upon her eyelids, if she closed her eyes, a dozen to each tender arc of flesh. They would gather on her face, around her nose and mouth. Clothlike, like rags and tatters, like large dry ashes of burnt cloth, they came in lazy droves, in fleets, sailing on the air. They were never in any hurry, being everywhere at once and always ready to bite. Nancy had been known to jump all the way out of the car and go stamping across the grass like a calf. She grew sulky and despairing and stood on one leg at a time in the moonlight, slapping at her ankles, while Rob leaned his chin on the doorframe and watched her with his affectionate, total interest.

Nancy, riddled and stinging with beads of actual blood briar-pointed here and there upon her, longed to be almost anywhere else—she especially longed for New Orleans. She always talked about it, although, never having been there, she had to say the things that other people said—food and jazz in the French Quarter, beer and crabs out on Lake Pontchartrain. Rob said vaguely they would go sometime. But she could tell that things were wrong for him at this point. "The food's just as good around here," he said.

"Oh, Rob!" She knew it wasn't so. She could feel that city, hanging just over the horizon from them scarcely fifty miles away, like some swollen bronze moon, at once brilliant and shadowy and drenched in every sort of amplified smell. Rob was stroking her hair, and in time his repeated, gentle touch gained her attention. It seemed to tell what he liked—girls all spanking clean, with scrubbed fingernails, wearing shoes still damp with white shoe polish. Even a fresh gardenia stuck in their hair wouldn't be too much for him. There would be all sorts of differences, to him, between Ship Island and the French Quarter, but she did not have much idea just what they were. Nancy took all this in, out of his hand on her head. She decided she had better not talk any more about New Orleans. She wriggled around, looking out over his shoulder, through the moonlight, toward where the pitch-black surface of the bayou water showed in patches through the trees. The trees were awful, hung with great spooky gray tatters of Spanish moss. Nancy was reminded of the house she and her family were living in; it had recently occurred to her that the peculiar smell it had must come from some Spanish moss that had got sealed in behind the paneling, between the walls. The moss was alive in there and growing, and that was where she was going to seal Bernard Nattier up someday, for him to see how it felt. She had tried to kill him once, by filling her purse with rocks and oyster shells—the roughest she could find. She had read somewhere that this weapon was effective for ladies in case of attack. But he had ducked when she swung the purse at him, and she had only gone spinning round and round, falling at last into a camellia tree, which had scratched her. . . .

"The Skeltons said for us to stop by there for a drink," Rob told her. They were driving again, and the car was back on the boulevard, in the still surprising daylight. "What did you say?" he asked her.

"Nothing."

"You just don't want to go?"

"No, I don't much want to go."

"Well, then, we won't stay long."

The Skelton house was right on the water, with a second-story, glassed-in, air-conditioned living room looking out over the sound. The sofas and chairs were covered with gold-and-white striped satin, and the room was full of Rob's friends. Lorna Skelton, who had been Rob's girl the summer before and who dressed so beautifully, was handing drinks round and saying, "So which is your favorite bayou, Rob?" She had a sort of fake "good sport" tone of voice and wanted to appear ready for anything. (Being so determined to be nice around Nancy, she was going to fall right over backward one day.)

"Do I have to have a favorite?" Rob asked. "They all look good to me. Full of slime and alligators."

"I should have asked Nancy."

"They're full of mosquitoes," said Nancy, hoping that was O.K. for an answer. She thought that virgins were awful people.

"Trapped, boy!" Turner Carmichael said to Rob, and banged him on the shoulder. Turner wanted to be a writer, so he thought it was all right to tell people about themselves. "Women will be your downfall, Acklen. Nancy, honey, you haven't spoken to the general."

Old General Skelton, Lorna's grandfather, sat in the corner of the living room near the mantel, drinking a scotch highball. You had to shout at him.

"How's the election going, General?" Turner asked.

"Election? Election? What election? Oh, the election! Well—" He lowered his voice, confidentially. As with most deaf people, his tone went to extremes. "There's no question of it. The one we want is the one we know. Know Houghman's father. Knew his grandfather. His stand is the same, identical one that we are all accustomed to. On every subject—this race thing especially. Very dangerous now. Extremely touchy. But Houghman—absolute! Never experiment, never question, never turn back. These are perilous times."

"Yes, sir," said Turner, nodding in an earnestly false way, which was better than the earnestly impressed way a younger boy at the general's elbow shouted, "General Skelton, that's just what my daddy says!"

"Oh yes," said the old man, sipping scotch. "Oh yes, it's true. And you, missy?" he thundered suddenly at Nancy, making her jump. "Are you just visiting here?"

"Why, Granddaddy," Lorna explained, joining them, "Nancy lives here now. You know Nancy."

"Then why isn't she tan?" the old man continued. "Why so pale and wan, fair nymph?"

"Were you a nymph?" Turner asked. "All this time?"

"For me I'm dark," Nancy explained. But this awkward way of putting it proved more than General Skelton could hear, even after three shoutings.

Turner Carmichael said, "We used to have this crazy colored girl who went around saying, 'I'se really white, 'cause all my chillun is,'" and of course *that* was what General Skelton picked to hear. "Party's getting rough," he complained.

"Granddaddy," Lorna cried, giggling, "you don't understand!"

"Don't I?" said the old gentleman. "Well, maybe I don't."

"Here, Nancy, come help me," said Lorna, leading her guest toward the kitchen.

On the way, Nancy heard Rob ask Turner, "Just where did you have this colored girl, did you say?"

"Don't be a dope. I said she worked for us."

"Aren't they a scream?" Lorna said, dragging a quart bottle of soda out of the refrigerator. "I thank God every night Granddaddy's deaf. You know, he was in the First World War and killed I don't know how many Germans, and he still can't stand to hear what he calls loose talk before a lady."

"I thought he was in the Civil War," said Nancy, and then of course she knew that that was the wrong thing and that Lorna, who just for an instant gave her a glance less than polite, was not going to forget it. The fact was, Nancy had never thought till that minute which war General Skelton had been in. She hadn't thought because she didn't care.

It had grown dark by now, and through the kitchen windows Nancy could see that the moon had risen—a moon in the clumsy stage, swelling between three-quarters and full, yet pouring out light on the water. Its rays were bursting against the long breakwater of concrete slabs, the remains of what the hurricane had shattered.

After saying such a fool thing, Nancy felt she could not stay in that kitchen another minute with Lorna, so she asked where she could go comb her hair. Lorna showed her down a hallway, kindly switching the lights on.

The Skeltons' bathroom was all pale blue and white, with handsome jars of rose bath salts and big fat scented bars of rosy soap. The lights came on impressively and the fixtures were heavy, yet somehow it all looked dead. It came to Nancy that she had really been wondering about just what would be in this sort of bathroom ever since she had seen those boys, with maybe Rob among them, playing tennis while she jumped on the trampoline. Surely the place had the air of an inner shrine, but what was there to see? The tops of all the bottles fitted firmly tight, and the soap in the tub was dry. Somebody had picked it all out—that was the point—judging soap and bath salts just the way they judged outsiders, business, real estate, politics. Nancy's father made judgments, too. Once, he argued all evening that Hitler was a well-meaning man; another time, he said the world was ready for communism. You could tell he was judging wrong, because he didn't have a bathroom like this one. Nancy's face in the mirror resembled a flower in a room that was too warm.

When she went out again, they had started dancing a little—a sort of friendly shifting around before the big glass windows overlooking the sound. General Skelton's chair was empty; he was gone. Down below, Lorna's parents could be heard coming in; her mother called upstairs. Her father appeared and shook hands all around. Mrs. Skelton soon followed him. He was wearing a white jacket, and she had on a silver cocktail dress with silver shoes. They looked like people in magazines. Mrs. Skelton held a crystal platter of things to eat in one hand, with a lace handkerchief pressed between the flesh and the glass in an inevitable sort of way.

In a moment, when the faces, talking and eating, the music, the talk, and the dancing swam to a still point before Nancy's eyes, she said, "You must all come to my house next week. We'll have a party."

A silence fell. Everyone knew where Nancy lived, in that cluster of old run-down houses the boulevard swept by. They knew that her house, especially, needed paint outside and furniture inside. Her daddy drank too much, and through her dress they could perhaps clearly discern the pin that held her slip together. Maybe, since they knew everything, they could look right through the walls of the house and see her daddy's donkey.

"Sure we will," said Rob Acklen at once. "I think that would be grand."

"Sure we will, Nancy," said Lorna Skelton, who was such a good sport and who was not seeing Rob this summer.

"A party?" said Turner Carmichael, and swallowed a whole anchovy. "Can I come, too?"

Oh, dear Lord, Nancy was wondering, what made me say it? Then she was on the stairs with her knees shaking, leaving the party, leaving with Rob to go down to Biloxi, where the two of them always went, and hearing the right things said to her and Rob, and smiling back at the right things but longing to jump off into the dark as if it were water. The dark, with the moon mixed in with it, seemed to her like good deep water to go off in.

She might have known that in the Marine Room of the Buena Vista down in Biloxi, they would run into more friends of Rob's. They always ran into somebody, and she might have known. These particular ones had already arrived and were even waiting for Rob, being somewhat bored in the process. It wasn't that Rob was so bright and witty, but he listened and liked everybody; he saw them the way they liked to be seen. So then they would go on to new heights, outdoing themselves, coming to believe how marvelous they really were. Two fraternity brothers of his were there tonight. They were sitting at a table with their dates—two tiny girls with tiny voices, like mosquitoes. They at once asked Nancy where she went to college, but before she could reply and give it away that her school so far had been only a cow college up in Arkansas and that she had gone there because her daddy couldn't afford anywhere else, Rob broke in and answered for her. "She's been in a finishing school in Little Rock," he said, "but I'm trying to talk her into going to the university."

Then the girls and their dates all four spoke together. They said, "Great!"

"Now watch," said one of the little girls, whose name was Teenie. "Cootie's getting out that little ole rush book."

Sure enough, the tiniest little notebook came out of the little cream silk bag of the other girl, who was called Cootie, and in it Nancy's name and address were written down with a sliver of a gold pencil. The whole routine was a fake, but a kind fake, as long as Rob was there. The minute those two got her into the ladies' room it would turn into another thing altogether; that she knew. Nancy knew all about mosquitoes. They'll sting me till I crumple up and die, she thought, and what will they ever care? So, when the three of them did leave the table, she stopped to straighten the strap of her shoe at the door to the ladies' room and let them go on through, talking on and on to one another about Rush Week. Then she went down a corridor and around a corner and down a short flight of steps. She ran down a long basement hallway where the service quarters were, past linen closets and cases of soft drinks, and, turning another corner and trying a door above a stairway, she came out, as she thought she would, in a nightclub place called the Fishnet, far away in the wing. It was a good place to hide; she and Rob had been there often. I can make up some sort of story later, she thought, and crept up on the last bar stool. Up above the bar, New Orleans-style (or so they said), a man was pumping tunes out of an electric organ. He wore rings on his chubby fingers and kept a handkerchief near him to mop his brow and to swab his triple chins with between songs. He waved his hand at Nancy. "Where's Rob, honey?" he asked.

She smiled but didn't answer. She kept her head back in the shadows. She wished only to be like another glass in the sparkling row of glasses lined up before the big gleam of mirrors and under the play of lights. What made me say that about a party? she kept wondering. To some people it would be nothing, nothing. But not to her. She fumbled in her bag for a cigarette. Inadvertently, she drank from a glass near her hand. The man sitting next to her smiled at her. "I didn't want it anyway," he said.

"Oh, I didn't mean—" she began. "I'll order one." Did you pay now? She rummaged in her bag.

But the man said, "What'll it be?" and ordered for her. "Come on now, take it easy," he said. "What's your name?"

"Nothing," she said, by accident.

She had meant to say Nancy, but the man seemed to think it was funny. "Nothing what?" he asked. "Or is it by any chance Miss Nothing? I used to know a large family of Nothings, over in Mobile."

"Oh, I meant to say Nancy."

"Nancy Nothing. Is that it?"

Another teaser, she thought. She looked away from his eyes, which glittered like metal, and what she saw across the room made her uncertainties vanish. She felt her whole self settle and calm itself. The man she had seen that morning on the beach wearing a red bandanna shirt and shorts was standing near the back of the Fishnet, looking on. Now he was wearing a white dinner jacket and a black tie, with a red cummerbund over his large stomach, but he was unmistakably the same man. At that moment, he positively seemed to Nancy to be her own identity. She jumped up and left the teasing man at the bar and crossed the room.

"Remember me?" she said. "I saw you on the beach this morning."

"Sure I do. You ran off when it started to rain. I had to run, too."

"Why did you?" Nancy asked, growing happier every minute.

"Because the rain was so hot it burnt me. If I could roll up my sleeve, I'd show you the blisters on my arm."

"I believe you. I had some, too, but they went away." She smiled, and the man smiled back. The feeling was that they would be friends forever.

"Listen," the man said after a while. "There's a fellow here you've got to meet now. He's out on the veranda, because it's too hot in here. Anyway, he gets tired just with me. Now you come on."

Nancy Lewis was always conscious of what she had left behind her. She knew that right now her parents and old Mrs. Poultney, with her rent collector's jaw, and Miss

Henriette Dupré, with her religious calf eyes, and the Nattiers, mother and son, were all sitting on the back porch in the half-light, passing the bottle of 6-12 around, and probably right now discussing the fact that Nancy was out with Rob again. She knew that when her mother thought of Rob her heart turned beautiful and radiant as a sea shell on a spring night. Her father, both at home and at his office, took his daughter's going out with Rob as excuse for saying something disagreeable about Rob's father, who was a big insurance man. There was always some talk about how Mr. Acklen had trickily got out of the bulk of his hurricane-damage payments, the same as all the other insurance men had done. Nancy's mother was probably responding to such a charge at this moment. "Now, you don't know that's true," she would say. But old Mrs. Poultney would say she knew it was true with her insurance company (implying that she knew but wouldn't say about the Acklen company, too). Half the house she was renting to the Lewises had blown right off it—all one wing—and the upstairs bathroom was ripped in two, and you could see the wallpapered walls of all the rooms, and the bathtub, with its pipes still attached, had got blown into the telephone wires. If Mrs. Poultney had got what insurance money had been coming to her, she would have torn down this house and built a new one. And Mrs. Nattier would say that there was something terrible to her about seeing wallpapered rooms exposed that way. And Miss Henriette Dupré would say that the Dupré house had come through it all ab-so-lootly intact, meaning that the Duprés had been foresighted enough to get some sort of special heavenly insurance, and she would be just longing to embark on explaining how they came by it, and she would, too, given a tenth of a chance. And all the time this went on, Nancy could see into the Acklens' house just as clearly—see the Acklens sitting inside their sheltered game room after dinner, bathed in those soft bug-repellent lights. And what were the Acklens saying (along with their kind of talk about their kind of money) but that they certainly hoped Rob wasn't serious about that girl? Nothing had to matter if he wasn't serious. . . . Nancy could circle around all of them in her mind. She could peer into windows, overhearing; it was the only way she could look at people. No human in the whole human world seemed to her exactly made for her to stand in front of and look squarely in the eye, the way she could look Bernard Nattier in the eye (he not being human either) before taking careful aim to be sure not to miss him with a purseful of rocks and oyster shells, or the way she could look this big man in the red cummerbund in the eye, being convinced already that he was what her daddy called a "natural." Her daddy liked to come across people he could call that, because it made him feel superior.

As the big man steered her through the crowded room, threading among the tables, going out toward the veranda, he was telling her his life story all along the way. It seemed that his father was a terribly rich Yankee who paid him not to stay at home. He had been in love with a policeman's daughter from Pittsburgh, but his father broke it up. He was still in love with her and always would be. It was the way he was; he couldn't help being faithful, could he? His name was Alfred, but everybody called him Bub. The fellow his father paid to drive him around was right down there, he said, as they stepped through the door and out on the veranda.

Nancy looked down the length of the veranda, which ran along the side of the hotel, and there was a man sitting on a bench. He had on a white jacket and was staring straight ahead, smoking. The highway curled around the hotel grounds, following the curve of the shore, and the cars came glimmering past, one by one, sometimes with lights on inside, sometimes spilling radio music that trailed up in long waves and met the electric-organ music coming out of the bar. Nancy and Bub walked toward the man. Bub counseled her gently, "His name is Dennis." Some people in full evening dress were coming up the divided walk before the hotel, past the canna lilies blooming deeply red under the high, powerful lights, where the bugs coned in long footless whirlpools. The people were drunk and laughing.

"Hi, Dennis," Bub said. The way he said it, trying to sound confident, told her that he was scared of Dennis.

Dennis's head snapped up and around. He was an erect, strong, square-cut man, not very tall. He had put water on his light brown hair when he combed it, so that it streaked light and dark and light again and looked like wood. He had cold eyes, which did not express anything—just the opposite of Rob Acklen's.

"What you got there?" he asked Bub.

"I met her this morning on the beach," Bub said.

"Been holding out on me?"

"Nothing like that," said Bub. "I just now saw her again."

The man called Dennis got up and thumbed his cigarette into the shrubbery. Then he carefully set his heels together and bowed. It was all a sort of joke on how he thought people here behaved. "Would you care to dance?" he inquired.

Dancing there on the veranda, Nancy noticed at once that he had a tense, strong wrist that bent back and forth like something manufactured out of steel. She also noticed that he was making her do whatever it was he called dancing; he was good at that. The music coming out of the Fishnet poured through the windows and around them. Dennis was possibly even thirty years old. He kept talking the whole time. "I guess he's told you everything, even about the policeman's daughter. He tells everybody everything, right in the first two minutes. I don't know if it's true, but how can you tell? If it wasn't true when it happened, it is now." He spun her fast as a top, then slung her out about ten feet—she thought she would certainly sail right on out over the railing and maybe never stop till she landed in the gulf, or perhaps go splat on the highway—but he got her back on the beat and finished up the thought, saying, "Know what I mean?"

"I guess so," Nancy said, and the music stopped.

The three of them sat down together on the bench. "What do we do now?" Dennis asked.

"Let's ask her," said Bub. He was more and more delighted with Nancy. He had been tremendously encouraged when Dennis took to her.

"You ask her," Dennis said.

"Listen, Nancy," Bub said. "Now, listen. Let me just tell you. There's so much money—that's the first thing to know. You've got no idea how much money there is. Really crazy. It's something, actually, that nobody knows—"

"If anybody knew," said Dennis, "they might have to tell the government."

"Anyway, my stepmother on this yacht in Florida, her own telephone—by radio, you know—she'd be crazy to meet you. My dad is likely off somewhere, but maybe not. And there's this plane down at Palm Beach, pilot and all, with nothing to do but go to the beach every day, just to pass away the time, and if he's not there for any reason, me and Dennis can fly just as good as we can drive. There's Alaska, Beirut—would you like to go to Beirut? I've always wanted to. There's anything you say."

"See that Cad out there?" said Dennis. "The yellow one with the black leather upholstery? That's his. I drive."

"So all you got to do," Bub told her, "is wish. Now, wait—now, think. It's important!" He all but held his hand over her mouth, as if playing a child's game, until finally he said, "Now! What would you like to do most in the world?"

"Go to New Orleans," said Nancy at once, "and eat some wonderful food."

"It's a good idea," said Dennis. "This dump is getting on my nerves. I get bored most of the time anyway, but today I'm bored silly."

"So wait here!" Nancy said. "So wait right here!"

She ran off to get Rob. She had all sorts of plans in her head. But Rob was all taken up. There were now more of his friends. The Marine Room was full of people just like him, lounging around two big tables shoved together, with about a million 7-Up bottles and soda bottles and glasses before them, and girls spangled among them, all silver, gold, and white. It was as if while Nancy was gone they had moved into mirrors to multiply themselves. They were talking to themselves about things she couldn't join in, any more than you can dance without feet. Somebody was going into politics, somebody was getting married to a girl who trained horses, somebody was just back from Europe. The two little mosquito girls weren't saying anything much any more; they had their little chins glued to their little palms. When anybody mentioned the university, it sounded like a small country the people right there were running *in absentia* to suit themselves. Last year's Maid of Cotton was there, and so, it turned out, was the girl horse trainer—tall, with a sheaf of upswept brown hair fastened with a glittering pin; she sat like the mast of a ship, smiling and talking about horses. Did she know personally every horse in the Southern states?

Rob scarcely looked up when he pulled Nancy in. "Where you been? What you want to drink?" He was having another good evening. He seemed to be sitting up above the rest, as though presiding, but this was not actually so; only his fondness for every face he saw before him made him appear to be raised a little, as if on a special chair.

And, later on, it seemed to Nancy that she herself had been, among them, like a person who wasn't a person— another order of creature passing among or even through them. Was it just that nothing, nobody, could really distract them when they got wrapped up in themselves?

"I met some people who want to meet you," she whispered to Rob. "Come on out with me."

"O.K.," he said. "In a minute. Are they from around here?"

"Come on, come on," she urged. "Come on out."

"In a minute," he said. "I will in a minute," he promised.

Then someone noticed her pulling at his sleeve, and she thought she heard Lorna Skelton laugh.

She went racing back to Bub and Dennis, who were waiting for her so docilely they seemed to be the soul of goodness, and she said, "I'll just ride around for a while, because I've never been in a Cadillac before." So they rode around and came back and sat for a while under the huge brilliant overhead lights before the hotel, where the bugs spiraled down. They did everything she said. She could make them do anything. They went to three different places, for instance, to find her some Dentyne, and when they found it they bought her a whole carton of it.

The bugs did a jagged frantic dance, trying to climb high enough to kill themselves, and occasionally a big one crashed with a harsh dry sound against the pavement. Nancy remembered dancing in the open air, and the rough salt feel of the air whipping against her skin as she spun fast against the air's drift. From behind she heard the resonant, constant whisper of the gulf. She looked toward the hotel doors and thought that if Rob came through she would hop out of the car right away, but he didn't come. A man she knew passed by, and she just all of a sudden said, "Tell Rob I'll be back in a minute," and he, without even looking up said, "O.K., Nancy," just like it really was O.K., so she said what the motor was saying, quiet but right there, and definitely running just under the splendid skin of the car, "Let's go on for a little while."

"Nancy, I think you're the sweetest girl I ever saw," said Bub, and they drove off.

She rode between them, on the front seat of the Cadillac. The top was down and the moon spilled over them as they rode, skimming gently but powerfully along the shore and the sound, like a strong rapid cloud traveling west. Nancy watched the point where the moon actually met the water. It was moving and still at once. She thought that it was glorious, in a messy sort of way. She would have liked to poke her head up out of the water right there. She could feel the water pouring back through her white-hair, her face slathering over with moonlight.

"If it hadn't been for that crazy rain," Bub kept saying, "I wouldn't have met her."

"Oh, shut up about that goofy rain," said Dennis.

"It was like being spit on from above," said Nancy.

The needle crept up to eighty or more, and when they had left the sound and were driving through the swamp, Nancy shivered. They wrapped her in a lap robe from the back seat and turned the radio up loud.

It was since she got back, since she got back home from New Orleans, that her mother did not put on the thin voile afternoon dress any more and serve iced tea to the neighbors on the back porch. Just yesterday, having nothing to do in the hot silence but hear the traffic stream by on the boulevard, and not wanting a suntan, and being certain the telephone would not ring, Nancy had taken some lemonade over to Bernard Nattier, who was sick in bed with the mumps. He and his mother had one room between them over at Mrs. Poultney's house, and they had stacks of magazines—the *Ladies' Home Journal*, *McCall's*, *Life*, and *Time*—piled along the walls. Bernard lay on a bunk bed pushed up under the window, in all the close heat, with no breeze able to come in at all. His face was puffed out and his eyes feverish. "I brought you some lemonade," said Nancy, but he said he couldn't drink it because it hurt his gums. Then he smiled at her, or tried to—it must have hurt even to do that, and it certainly made him look silly, like a cartoon of himself, but it was sweet.

"I love you, Nancy," he said, most irresponsibly.

She thought she would cry. She had honestly tried to kill him with those rocks and oyster shells. He knew that very well, and he, from the moment he had seen her, had set out to make her life one long torment, so where could it come from, a smile like that, and what he said? She didn't know. From the fever, maybe. She said she loved him, too.

Then, it was last night, just the night before, that her father had got drunk and made speeches beginning, "To think that a daughter of mine . . ." Nancy had sat through it all crouched in the shadows on the stair landing, in the very spot where the moss or old seaweed back of the paneling smelled the strongest and dankest, and thought of her mother upstairs, lying, clothed, straight out on the bed in the dark, with a headache and no cover on and maybe the roof above her melted away. Nancy looked down to where her father was marching up to the donkey that said, "If you really want to look like me—Just keep right on talking," and was picking it up and throwing it down, right on the floor. She cried out, before she knew it—"Oh!"—seeing him do the very thing she had so often meant to do herself. Why had he? Why? Because the whiskey had run out on him? Or because he had got too much of it again? Or from trying to get in one good lick at everything there was? Or because the advice he loved so much seemed now being offered to him?

But the donkey did not break. It lay there, far down in the tricky shadows; Nancy could see it lying there, looking back over its shoulder with its big red grinning mouth, and teeth like piano keys, still saying the same thing, naturally. Her father was tilting uncertainly down toward it, unable, without falling flat on his face, to reach it. This made a problem for him, and he stood thinking it all over, taking every aspect of it well into account, even though the donkey gave the impression that not even with a sledgehammer would it be broken, and lay as if on some deep distant sea floor, toward which all the sediment of life was drifting, drifting, forever slowly down. . . .

Beirut! It was the first time she had remembered it. They had said they would take her there, Dennis and Bub, and then she had forgotten to ask, so why think of it right now, on the street uptown, just when she saw Rob Acklen coming along? She would have to see him sometime, she guessed, but what did Beirut have to do with it?

"Nancy Lewis," he said pleasantly, "you ran out on me. Why did you act like that? I was always nice to you."

"I told them to tell you," she said. "I just went to ride around for a while."

"Oh, I got the word, all right. About fifty different people saw you drive off in that Cadillac. Now about a hundred claim to have. Seems like everybody saw those two characters but me. What did you do it for?"

"I didn't like those Skeltons, all those people you know. I didn't like those sorority girls, that Teenie and Cootie.

You knew I didn't, but you always took me where they were just the same."

"But the point is," said Rob Acklen, "I thought you liked me."

"Well, I did," said Nancy Lewis, as though it all had happened a hundred years ago. "Well, I did like you just fine."

They were still talking on the street. There had been the tail of a storm that morning, and the palms were blowing. There was a sense of them streaming like green flags above the low town.

Rob took Nancy to the drugstore and sat at a booth with her. He ordered her a fountain Coke and himself a cup of coffee. "What's happened to you?" he asked her.

She realized then, from what he was looking at, that something she had only half noticed was certainly there to be seen—her skin, all around the edges of her white blouse, was badly bruised and marked, and there was the purplish mark on her cheekbone she had more or less powdered over, along with the angry streak on her neck.

"You look like you fell through a cotton gin," Rob Acklen continued, in his friendly way. "You're not going to say the rain over in New Orleans is just scalding hot, are you?"

"I didn't say anything," she returned.

"Maybe the mosquitoes come pretty big over there," he suggested. "They wear boxing gloves, for one thing, and, for another—"

"Oh, stop it, Rob," she said, and wished she was anywhere else.

It had all stemmed from the moment down in the French Quarter, over late drinks somewhere, when Dennis had got nasty enough with Bub to get rid of him, so that all of Dennis's attention from that point onward had gone exclusively to Nancy. This particular attention was relentless and direct, for Dennis was about as removed from any sort of affection and kindness as a human could be. Maybe it had all got boiled out of him; maybe he had never had much to get rid of. What he had to say to her was nothing she hadn't heard before, nothing she hadn't already been given more or less to understand from mosquitoes, people, life-in-general, and the rain out of the sky. It was just that he said it in a final sort of way—that was all.

"I was in a wreck," said Nancy.

"Nobody killed, I hope," said Rob.

She looked vaguely across at Rob Acklen with pretty, dark blue eyes that seemed to be squinting to see through shifting lights down in the deep sea; for in looking at him, in spite of all he could do, she caught a glimmering impression of herself, of what he thought of her, of how soft her voice always was, her face like a warm flower.

"I was doing my best to be nice to you. Why wasn't that enough?"

"I don't know," she said.

"None of those people you didn't like were out to get you. They were all my friends."

When he spoke in this handsome, sincere, and democratic way, she had to agree; she had to say she guessed that was right.

Then he said, "I was having such a good summer. I imagined you were, too," and she thought, He's coming down deeper and deeper, but one thing is certain—if he gets down as far as I am, he'll drown.

"You better go," she told him, because he had said he was on his way up to Shreveport on business for his father. And because Bub and Dennis were back; she'd seen them drift by in the car twice, once on the boulevard and once in town, silenter than cloud, Bub in the back, with his knees propped up, reading a magazine.

"I'll be going in a minute," he said.

"You just didn't realize I'd ever go running off like that," Nancy said, winding a damp Coca-Cola straw around her finger.

"Was it the party, the one you said you wanted to give? You didn't have to feel—"

"I don't remember any party," she said quickly.

Her mother lay with the roof gone, hands folded. Nancy felt that people's mothers, like wallpapered walls after a hurricane, should not be exposed. Her father at last successfully reached the donkey, but he fell in the middle of the rug, while Nancy, on the stair landing, smelling seaweed, asked herself how a murderous child with swollen jaws happened to mention love, if love is not a fever, and the storm-driven sea struck the open reef and went roaring skyward, splashing a tattered gull that clutched at the blast—but if we will all go there immediately it is safe in the Dupré house, because they have this holy candle. There are hidden bone-cold lairs no one knows of, in rock beneath the sea. She shook her bone-white hair.

Rob's whole sensitive face tightened harshly for saying what had to come next, and she thought for a while he wasn't going to make it, but he did. "To hell with it. To absolute hell with it then." He looked stricken, as though he had managed nothing but damaging himself.

"I guess it's just the way I am," Nancy murmured. "I just run off sometimes."

Her voice faded in a deepening glimmer where the human breath is snatched clean away and there are only bubbles, iridescent and pure. When she dove again, they rose in a curving track behind her.